THE BASS PLAYER

By Jim Reilly

For My Dad

PREPARING THE SPACE

Where do we start?

With nothing.

A blank page, a clean slate, an open book, silence.

No sound, just potential.

Advances from expectations.

Nowhere.

We start nowhere and then go. We must begin nowhere. There is no alternative.

Nowhere, nowhere, nowhere, now here.

Let's begin...

TUNING UP

By way of introduction, this is more or less how we hear:

Air is set in motion by a vibrating object. This could be anything, a string, vocal chord, glass shattering on the ground, anything that moves disrupts the air, sets it in motion and causes sound. The ear, with its unique cup like folds, intercepts this moving air and channels it through a short canal to a thin membrane stretched across the ear canal. This membrane, the eardrum, vibrates in rhythm with the air's vibrations. The eardrum transfers this motion to a group of small bones, which move in sympathy with fluctuations in pressure originally caused by the moving air. These small bones transform the physical, tangible air movements onto a coiled tube within the ear, which contains thousands of hair-like nerve endings. From there, the motion caused by the vibrating objects transform into electrical impulses, which the brain then decodes and identifies as sound.

What we perceive as a single sound is an incredibly complex combination of things. Think of a rock thrown into a pond. Ripples, waves radiate out from the point where the rock broke the water's surface. The ripples are what sound waves would look like if our eyes could see such things. You could think of the rock as the thing producing the sound.

We differentiate between the different types of sound waves by comparing their relative length. The length refers to the time it takes for the wave to go from its highest point through its lowest point and back again. Like a wave in the ocean, reaching its crest, falling, then rising again.

Any sound, except for the purest tones—a birdcall or the highest notes of a flute—consists of several sound waves of differing lengths occurring simultaneously. The ear hears the longest wave as the lowest note and compares the other waves to it. Thus, the quality of the sound as a whole is determined by a comparison of all the shorter, higher pitched waves, to the lowest portion of the sound. The nature of the entire sonic moment at hand is decided by the lowest, the deepest portion of the sound. Music theorists call this the fundamental. Musicians call this the root.

The tangible quality of the musical instant can therefore be defined as the relationship between the higher portions of the sound waves as they compare to the lowest, the longest wave. In other words, the very nature of the sound itself owes it quality—good, bad, or indifferent—to lowest note or part of that note.

The lowest note drives the bus.

The bass player plays the lowest notes.

WARMING UP

I first met him when I was a frustrated young musician. I had heard from a friend of a friend that he'd be in town and found out the hotel they were playing. It was a two-week residency. I had time and settled in for the duration.

I was there for the first night and had no plan really so I just sat at the back and listened. Mostly I just closed my eyes and let the music wash over me. The whole quartet was stellar - drums, piano, sax - but I was there for the bass player. It's hard for me to describe what it was like hearing him live for the first time. I had tons of his recordings of course, on CD and vinyl. I liked the vinyl, not surprisingly. The scratches and pops gave the music warmth that the digital re-issues couldn't touch. Dirt and grit added life.

But as I sat there with my eyes closed in the back of that small hotel bar, so small that they really didn't need any amplification, I wasn't ready for what I felt. I *felt* music for the first time. As he set the air in motion with his scarred, well-worn double bass (I knew the history of the instrument, or at least the myths of the instrument by then too) those vibrations at first enveloped me. Then it was as if my skin started vibrating in rhythm with his playing. Soon the music had invaded my whole body; I was a part of it. It was as if there was no separation, no empty space between musician, music and listener. We were one. It was beautiful. That hasn't happened since, at least not so strongly, but I'm still trying and hopeful.

Once again, it's hardly surprising that my first live encounter with his playing was anything less than transcendental. I had been building it up for years. He was my hero. Such a good musician but content, or so I thought, to sit at the back, out of the spotlight. He made other players sound better and in my mind, he never cared that those at the front of the stage took all the credit.

But how many times do you build something up only to be let down? How often does reality pale in comparison to the fantasies we've created? This wasn't one of those times. Hearing him live, in real time for the first time, being in the same space for the creation of his music changed me.

I had already decided that at some point I would introduce myself to him, ask for an autograph, hopefully not embarrass myself with the usual hero-worshipping. But after that first night, it was different. I could no longer be yet another one of the typical fans. There was more to it than that. His music existed on a different level and I had no idea how to come to terms with it or what to do next. I went the next night but I didn't listen. I watched. I watched as he closed his eyes and drifted off into the music. His hands, so big they made the ebony neck of his old German bass with the maple back and spruce top look like almost like a toy. They seemed to float above the strings, the epitome of grace and effortlessness. He never once opened his eyes. The right notes were always there. Ever silent, all the spaces between the notes breathed.

I went every night, but never found the nerve to go up to him after one of the shows. I wouldn't have known what to say anyway.

I continued being a frustrated musician. I hit the woodshed, inspired, and I got better and better. I closed my eyes more when I played. I listened, I felt, I trusted more and more that my hands, my fingers would find the right notes. More often than not, they did.

A few months after his residency, I was playing a club downtown. Not the same one he had played in, but it could have been - same small room, same type of crowd, same mixture of people getting the music and those who were clueless. I played well, or at least it felt like I played well. The music flowed. No epiphanies, no transcendent moments where the music pulled me out of my body and carried me off into the either, but it felt good and I was happy.

As I packed up and made my way, carrying my bass in front of me and being careful not to run into one of the low standing tables or hit someone's leg, through the thinning crowd to the door at the opposite side of the room, I saw him. My eyes were closed for most of the gig, but I wouldn't have seen him anyway. It was too dark to see from the stage to the back of the room. If he had been there all night I would never have known. I'm not sure I would have been able to play if I had known he was listening.

I was standing right in front of him, my bass between the two of us, before I realized that it was really him and he was looking right at me. I froze.

"You're good," he said. His voice low and growling, like his bass lines on the faster, darker tunes.

It was only seconds I'm sure but it felt like a lifetime before I mumbled, "Um, thanks. Uh that means a lot coming from you."

"Shit man, I'm nothing. Not a player tonight, just here to listen."

He didn't ask me to, but I sat down, leaned my bass against the wall, looked at him incredulously and blurted out, "Are you fucking kidding me?"

I sat with him for the rest of the night. We drank. I paid. As last call came and went, it became clearer and clearer that the night was wrapping up. Desperate not to let the moment end I asked, "So what are you doing here anyway?"

"I had nothing after those gigs I did here a couple of months ago. I got a couple of friends that I've stayed with and have picked up a couple of session gigs. TV cues, boring as shit but they pay, so I've stayed. You were at those gigs, weren't you?"

Holy fuck, seriously? How could he possibly have known or remembered me? "Um, ya," I said. "Really, you remember me?"

"Ya, I always check out the audience, and remember those who stand out. You should have told me you were a player."

Whether it was alcohol, or the new bravado inspired by him calling me a 'player' I don't know, but before I knew what I was saying I asked, "Well, if you're here for a while, how about a lesson?"

Silence.

And more silence. And I thought I had blown it. Then slowly, he drew a long breath in and let it out again. "Shit, I ain't no teacher, never have been never wanted to be." He had no idea how much he had already taught me. "But come down to the studio tomorrow and you can hang out if you want.

And so, it started. We hung out. And it took a while, but eventually he started telling me his story. At first little bits and pieces just kind of came out. Little stories about musicians he had played with, I'd asked him about some famous or infamous thing and he'd always laugh a little and say, "Shit it ain't nothing like that" and then he'd set the record straight.

After a couple of weeks, he said, "Shit boy, you writing a book or something? All these questions. Damn, you gonna write my book or something?"

We laughed, but something stuck.

It was about six months later. He had moved on. A call came in for another gig. A little over a month of steady road work in Europe. The kind of gigs he loved. Small rooms, audiences who know music. Lots of closed eyes. The bus was older but in good shape. It was winter though, and the roads should have been closed. I read about the crash in Downbeat, there was no real Internet yet.

"All those damn questions," he said. "You gonna write my book?"

Years later, that's exactly what I did. I sat down, and wrote down all I could remember, all that he told me. I have no idea how much of it is true. Most of it I guess, but who knows. It doesn't matter much anyway. The story is good and they're his stories anyway. Even though these are my words, I've done my best to let the stories remain his.

He wasn't famous, at least not the kind of famous that people write about, but players knew him. The people who hear past the music knew who he was and those who don't should. Close your eyes and read. He would have liked me saying that, he would understand.

I'm still a frustrated musician by the way. Even though I'm more famous than he ever was, I'll always be frustrated. Although I never would have believed it at the time, he was frustrated too. We all are.

FIRST SET

I. From the moment he was old enough to ask, his mother had told him that his father had died in the War. She told him that they were high school sweethearts, married at nineteen, the day before he was shipped overseas. She claimed that exactly (to the day) nine months after their wedding night he was born. When he was a little older, she added that he had been born around nine in the morning, and that later that same day, around three in the afternoon (she couldn't remember the exact time) a telegraph arrived saying that his father had been killed.

"So," she said, "you had a Daddy for about seven hours."

Even after he realized that the dates didn't line up (the War began about eight months after he was born) he never questioned her or pointed out the holes in her story. Even when she would tell the story to others. She'd talk about his father all the time, when she sat around the kitchen table with her girlfriends smoking long, filtered cigarettes, the smoke tinged with a hint of mint. To strangers on the bus when they made any sort of comment about the cute little boy clinging to her hip. Throughout his own life, when asked, he told others about his dad—Private First-Class Michael Jon Fraser—killed in the War the day he—Jon Michael Fraser—was born.

"Tell me another story about Daddy," Jon Michael Fraser, four years old, curls up on his mother's lap. It's just past 8:30 in the evening,

'Jack Teagarden and His Band Live From the Blackhawk Café' has begun, broadcasting every week on Radio W.B.E.Z. The two nestle closer, she reaches over and turns up the radio. Not too loud, not loud enough to distract her young son, just loud enough to drown out any other background noise: a couple passing on the street, the old couple arguing upstairs perhaps.

"Tell me another story about Daddy," little Jonny asks again, this time softer. He feels her breasts on his shoulder, her warm breath weaves through his hair.

"Your Daddy was the best violin player in the whole world," she almost whispers, her eyes staring out into the music as it drifts around the room, up to the ceiling, over to the corner then down and out in front of them, spreading out, getting ready for the embrace.

"LIVE FROM THE WORLD-FAMOUS BLACKHAWK CAFÉ . . . JACK TEAGARDEN AND HIS BAND..." the radio voice announces.

"Your Daddy used to come by my house after school, in the winter when it was dark early, take out his violin and play to me from the street in front of the house."

A RHYTHM SECTION INTRO, THREE CHORD VAMP (PIANO, DRUMS AND BASS)... TEAGARDEN SPEAKS *"THANK YOU LADIES AND GENTLEMEN, MY NAME IS JACK TEAGARDEN AND IT IS MY GREAT PLEASURE TO PERFORM FOR YOU THIS EVENING..."*

"Before *my* Daddy got home around seven, *your* Daddy used to come by and play for just me. Every other woman in the neighbourhood would stop what they were doing and listen to your father play. Everyone was in love with him. I think most of them dreamed that he was playing for them but he played only for me. He told me so on our wedding night."

THE BAND JOINS IN FIVE SAXES, THREE TROMBONES, THREE TRUMPETS, DRUMS BASS, GUITAR, PIANO, TEAGARDEN ON TROMBONE AND VOCALS. IT'S ALMOST TOO MUCH FOR THE LITTLE RADIO SPEAKER TO HANDLE AND THE SOUND DISTORTS JUST A LITTLE AROUND THE EDGES...

"I think even your grandmother had a little crush on him. She would never go outside and shoo him away until exactly a quarter to seven, and only then because your grandfather was on his way home."

"When will I meet Grandma and Grandpa?" Jon Michael interrupts, his eyes focused on the same spot as his mother's.

"Soon baby, soon."

TROMBONE SOLO, TEAGARDEN IS REALLY COOKING TONIGHT...

"Once, your grandfather came home early. Your Daddy was still in front of the house playing for me. The whole neighbourhood was lost in your Daddy's music. He used to make it up as he went along you know. Everybody must have had their eyes closed and was dreaming about the music that your Daddy was playing.

When you closed your eyes and listened to him, you could see pictures in your head. I'm not lying, it's true. Everybody's eyes were

16

closed and nobody saw or heard your grandfather come home. All of a sudden, your Daddy stopped playing in the middle of a beautiful high note and turned around to see your grandfather standing right behind him.

Everybody's eyes popped open at the same time and there was your Daddy and Grandpa standing facing each other. Your Daddy's violin hung by his side. Grandpa had the cane he used to help him walk, he was holding it in the middle, like he was going to hit your father. Grandma dropped the dish she was drying as she stood, watching through the kitchen window."

"'Are you playing for my daughter?' Grandpa asked.

"'Yes Sir, I am. I intend to marry her, Sir.' Your Daddy was the bravest man in world.

"Well, then," your grandpa spoke slowly, carefully, his voice flat, between cool and warm. 'You had better finish playing and come inside. You may introduce yourself properly to my little girl.'"

"THANK YOU, LADIES AND GENTLEMEN. FOR OUR NEXT NUMBER WE WOULD LIKE TO DO OUR OWN ARRANGEMENT OF..."

She leaned over slightly, looked down at her son. His chest was moving slowly, up then down, in then out. She hadn't noticed when he had fallen asleep.

They stayed like that for the rest of the evening, till around 3:00 am, when the static on the radio woke her and she carried little Jon Michael Fraser off to bed.

II. When he looked back on his childhood, as he often did, especially as he got older, he could never remember wanting. He never remembered his mother working, yet they were never short of cash. He never remembered being hungry or feeling alone. There was no constant parade of men revolving through their small, two-bedroom apartment at the corner of 12th Avenue and Cottonwood Drive. The neighbourhood was nice. There was a small park, half a block away, where the other kids gathered to play. A butcher, baker and green grocer were all within walking distance. On weekends, they would take the streetcar downtown and go to the theatre or stop by *Olsen's Delicatessen* for cool drinks in the summer, warm ones in the winter.

Their apartment was sparse yet functional. Three story building, stairs leading up from the street, two doors on each landing led into opposite apartments. Theirs' was on the second floor, right-hand side as you came up from the street. This wasn't the first place they had lived. He remembered another, shadows mostly, a dark place, noisy. He doesn't remember light coming through windows until they moved to this place.

The landlord sold her on the apartment when he said, "You don't even need to heat it. You're surrounded on all sides. Your neighbours will take care of your heating bills for you."

She nodded as if heat wasn't an issue, "Are the neighbours quiet?" she asked. "We're a very quiet couple. Little Jonny here hasn't cried once since the day he was born. I kid you not."

"Oh yea, no problem," replied the man. He was wearing a dark suit. "If you're done looking around, I have got to get back to work. Do you want the place or not?"

"Well," his mother replied. "It is a little small and there is a bit of a draft. If you promise to replace those curtains, we'll take it." Quickly she added, "It's only temporary you know, just till we get back on our feet."

"Of course," said the man, "only temporary."

There were four rooms: a kitchen/dining room, a living room and two bedrooms. The door from the outside hallway entered into the kitchen. Icebox on the left, counter, sink on the right separated by a small, clean gas stove. The dining room was an extension on the kitchen, the same red tile floor covered both. A doorway led into the living room and two doors from the living room led to the bedrooms. The doorframe between the kitchen and the living room had marks where a door had been removed. The doors were still in place on the bedrooms.

Three windows looked out on the outside world. The living room window was larger and had a small balcony off it. Not large enough to sit on, even for little Jonny, but a row of flowers or maybe some cooking herbs would fit nicely. (She made a mental note to start her garden right away.) The bedroom windows were simpler and looked onto the drive not the avenue. In truth, they were just small, square holes cut into the side of the building after it had been completed. The holes with glass fitted as an afterthought. No one noticed the bedrooms were windowless until people started moving in. After some debate, the holes were cut and glassed in. Most appreciated the little bit of sunlight in the morning.

They had a table, rectangular with four chairs, a matching set, in the dining area. A couch sat against the wall that separated the kitchen from the living room. The radio sat within arm's distance beside the couch. It didn't sit in front of the couch against an opposite wall like most of Jonny's friend's radios were set up.

"It's just a box," his mom always said. "You don't have to look at it to make it work."

There were lamps in opposite corners, a small painting of the Canadian Rockies on one wall and a plant beside the window.

The bedrooms were exactly the same size. She took the one on the corner, the one on both 12th and Cottonwood. Jon's room was sandwiched between his mother's and the rest of the apartment, facing only the side street. The arrangement made him feel safe. Both rooms had the same size beds—singles—each bed pressed tight against their respective right-hand walls (as you walked in). Lamps on nightstands stood beside each bed, small chests of drawers three drawers high stood on the left walls opposite the beds. Her room was painted a light red. His gentle blue.

This was Jonny's home until he left about twelve years later. Little changed during those twelve years. The plant was replaced a few times. It was Jonny's job to water it and he often forgot. She would let it die to teach him a lesson, then replace it with another plant and put it in exactly the same place. The space was never empty long. Jonny would go to school, the plant irretrievably brown. When he got home it would be green and alive again.

The Rockies never moved. When he was bored Jonny would pretend that it wasn't a picture at all but another little window. Mom sometimes did the same thing. She never managed to start a little garden on the balcony.

III. The closest high school to their apartment was called Presidents Memorial. They couldn't decide which president to name it after so they decided to include them all. A few years after Jonny had been there, they almost renamed it after JFK. But by the time they got around to debating, fourteen other schools in the state had already been renamed JFK. They didn't want to be seen as jumping on a bandwagon.

It was a red brick building, two floors, stone steps leading up to the front entrance, the rest of the school spreading out like a narrow horseshoe from the front doors. Immediately in front of the main entrance were the administration offices and on either side staircases led to the second floors. On both top and bottom floors twelve classrooms, six each side, stretched down a long, narrow corridor. The floors were red tile, like in Jonny's kitchen, more worn of course but pretty much the same colour. The colour made it feel homey, comfortable to him. Two times twelve—twenty-four rooms on each floor, two times twenty-four—forty-eight rooms total.

The school was built five years before Fraser was old enough to attend. The city planners intentionally built it too large. The first year only twenty-eight rooms were in constant use. By the time Fraser arrived, they were using close to forty. Eighth and ninth grades used the bottom floor, tenth, eleventh and twelfth the top.

Jon Michael Fraser was tall for his age. He had always been long (like his father) constantly mistaken for being a couple of years older than he actually was. Tall, but thin. Tall and thin, with long, beautiful fingers that seemed to stretch out and wrap around whatever he grabbed. His hands looked like spiders, like daddy longlegs, little bodies and long, spindly legs. Even when he was young he could pick up a baseball, get a good grip and throw, without the ball ever touching the palm of his hand.

The music room at Presidents Memorial was on the second floor, down the right wing, last door, (the sixth one) on the left. All grades used the same room. There was no division by age. At the time, there were not enough students to divide them by ability either. Twelve-year-old Jon sat beside seventeen-year-old William Perry. It made no real difference though. Most of the student musicians had only been playing for a couple of years regardless of their age and for the most part none could really play.

"We need two trumpets, one trombone, six clarinets, one violin, two cellos, snare drum and cymbals."

Jon looked up to see a tall, thin man (much like himself) standing at the front of the class.

"New students, come to the front of the class for your instruments. Returning students, you'll play the same instruments you played last year." A collective groan came up from the returning students. Jon made his way to the front of the room with seven others: six boys and one girl, not all the openings would be filled.

Mr. William David Redfern, 'Instructor of Music and Physical Education' at Presidents Memorial High School greeted each new student and checked their name against a class list as each made their way to the front of the class.

"Name?" Redfern said.

"Age?

"Have you ever played a musical instrument before?

"Thank you, go to the back of the room and pick up case number (insert case # here), your (insert instrument type here) is inside."

It was a speech William Redfern was used to saying. He had learned his craft, trumpet, playing in the garrison band during the war. He returned home, minus the last two fingers on his left hand, and headed straight for New Orleans. His crippled hand didn't affect his playing though. Physically anyway. His right hand was still fine. He could hold his trumpet without difficulty in his left and finger with more than average dexterity in his right.

He got to New Orleans on a hot, wet August night and went straight out to the streets he and the other musicians in the garrison would stay up late at night and dream about. He walked into the loudest, smokiest bar he could find, his trumpet tucked under his arm. One step through the door and the place turned quiet. Every dark eye turned and looked at him. He felt a hot, a steaming hot, bead of sweat fall from his jaw and land on his crippled left hand. It burned like acid. He turned and ran. North for days until he ended up at Presidents High.

He still played as much as he could, sitting in for many of the better social bands in town and leading his own small group. Redfern

24

sensed the end of the big bands and a shift to small groups was on its way. He figured he would be ready when it happened. Maybe he could even find the right guys and play enough to not have to bother with teaching anymore. Maybe.

"Name?"

"Jon Michael Fraser, Sir."

"Age?"

"Twelve, almost thirteen Sir."

"Have you ever played a musical instrument before?"

"No Sir, but my Father played violin."

"Where's your father now? Does he still play?"

"No Sir, he was killed in the war Sir."

"Killed in the war, eh?"

"Yes sir."

"What was his name then?"

"Michael Jon Fraser, Sir, just like mine but in a different order."

"Yes, clever," Redfern thought for a moment. "Well, I've never heard of him. Violin eh?'

"Yes sir," Fraser looked towards the floor.

"All right, go to the back of the room and pick up case number 11, your violin is inside."

"Thank you, Sir."

"Name..."

IV. "Fraser!"

"Yes sir?"

"Come here, there's someone I would like you to meet."

Jon Michael Fraser's growth on his violin was out-matched only by his physical growth. In the two years since Mr. Redfern had given him his violin, Fraser had grown over six inches. He now measured six feet even. He was fifteen.

"Fraser, this is Mr. Clayton. He's the president of our local musicians' union. Do you know what that is Fraser?"

Jon knew, of course he knew, he even knew Clayton. Last year Clayton had stopped by the school about this same time. He overheard Clayton and Redfern talking about last year's batch of student musicians. From what Jon remembered, their conversation had gone something like:

> Clayton: *"Any of those little shits hold their own in the real world?"*
>
> Redfern: *"Ha, no, not yet, a couple are close but right now, like lambs to the slaughter."*

"No sir, I am not sure." Fraser lied.

Clayton took over. "*The American Federation of Musicians* boy. I am the president of the local chapter. No musician - none who want to get paid anyway - works in this town without going through me."

Something bordering on respect began to replace Fraser's original sarcasm.

"Mr. Redfern here has told me that you are one of his many prized students," Clayton continued.

Fraser tried to count the other prized students, but got stuck at one. He kept that thought to himself. "I try my best sir," he replied.

"Can you read?" Clayton asked.

"Yes, sir." There was nothing Redfern had given Fraser that he hadn't been able to work his way through.

"I mean sight read boy, can you read on the bandstand?"

"I don't know sir, I can read most everything right away if that's what you mean."

This was true.

"Yes, that is what I mean. Have you played in front of an audience?" Clayton was beginning to sound annoyed. He pronounced each word tightly, with sharp edges. His face took on a reddish hue.

This answer was a little trickier. Of course, there had been six school concerts in the two years Fraser had been at Presidents Memorial. Those would be the only performances he would mention. He wouldn't mention the performances for his mother.

When he first came home with his violin his mother wept.

"I thought you would be proud. I want to be just like my Father," Fraser cried out, nearly in tears himself.

Rather than answer, his Mother buried her face in her hands and sobbed uncontrollably. The old man from upstairs came down to see what was the matter. Fraser answered the door and told the nosy neighbour that everything was alright. Seeing that no one seemed injured, he went back upstairs but kept his ear open for any sounds of more serious trouble.

At first, Jon would practice as quietly as he could, in his room, after he was supposed to go sleep. His mother would tuck him in then go back to the living room and turn up *The Nine O'clock Music Hour* on Radio W.B.E.Z. He would climb silently out of bed and practice his fingerings. Left hand only, no bow, no sound. He could practice with the bow at school.

First finger - Second finger - Third finger - Fourth
First - Second - Fourth
First - Third - Fourth.
All strings; then shift positions up and down the neck.

Fifty-five minutes later, he would slide his violin under his bed and crawl back under the covers. Sometimes he would already be asleep when she came in to kiss him on the forehead before she went to bed herself. Other times, he would still be awake. Music still swirling through his head.

As he lay in bed, he could see glorious jets of colour shooting up into the sky as his mind chased his notes up into the heavens. Then, a quick turn of his wrist and down would come the sounds in his head, crashing like waterfalls, cascading down great heights, tearing into the ground below and careening off into millions of tiny drops of mist, landing gently on a rose petal or fresh green leaf.

Sometimes his Mother's kiss would be a part of his unconscious symphony sending him off on another run of colour, light and sound. Sometimes the spot she kissed would feel like an opening. An opening where all this light and colour and sound would pour out and into the world. Other times her kiss would catch him off guard and the music would disappear. When he tried to recreate it after she left he was never able to.

For almost six months, he hid his violin from her. Then one day she left him home alone. Just for a minute, to go to the green grocer. As the door closed he went to his room. Now he could practice with his bow. He was gone with the first down-stroke.

Forty-five minutes later he was back. He looked at the clock on his bedside table, dropped his violin and bow on the bed and ran out into the living room. His Mother was sitting on the couch, he could see a bag of groceries on the kitchen table. The radio was turned on, the dial glowed its usual light amber but the sound was turned down.

"I pretended it was the radio," she said. "It was the only way I could keep from disturbing you. You sound better than anything on the radio anyway."

He just stared at her. Her eyes looked out into the space that was usually filled by W.B.E.Z.'s *Live In Studio Broadcast of...* His mouth opened as if to speak, her head turned as if to look. He just turned, went back to his room and played for his Mother.

"Well boy, have you ever played in front of real people," Clayton was growing tired now.

"Ah, ya, yes a, sir, yes, I have played in all the school concerts. Last fall, I had first chair and took two solos."

Clayton stepped back and looked Jon Michael Fraser over from top to bottom. "I have a couple of small groups who are in need of a violin. Can you keep your mouth shut, your ears open and follow directions?"

"Yes sir, I can."

"Then come to this address this evening," Clayton handed him a business card, white with black, embossed lettering. "And bring your father," Clayton added, "I can't use a minor without a parent's signature."

"My Father was killed in the War, Sir," Fraser replied quickly.

"Who do you live with then?" Clayton's face twisted.

"My Mother, sir."

"Then bring your goddamn Mother, it makes no difference to me." Clayton turned to leave.

"Yes sir," Fraser called after him. "You didn't say what time, sir?" Fraser was yelling now, walking quickly after Mr. Clayton.

"Seven o'clock and don't be late or you'll never work in this town again." Clayton was smiling, but his back was to Fraser.

"Yes sir, seven o'clock sharp. I ... ah ...we ... will be there..."

V. He expected to have a difficult time persuading his mother to take him down to the hall to see Mr. Clayton. He had prepared a lie. He planned to tell her that Mr. Redfern had arranged for each student to spend an evening at the musician's Union Hall. A sort of 'see how the pros do it' type of expedition.

Jon walked up the stairs from the street, through the door that entered into the kitchen, then on through to the living room. His Mother sat on the couch, radio on: *News*.

Mother turned and smiled, "How's my baby?" she asked, the edges of her mouth pulled up, her eyes brightened.

He couldn't lie. "I'm good," he said as he let out his breath.

He told his Mother about Mr. Clayton and about the A. F. of M. and about how good he was getting and about how everybody wanted him to play with them and about how much he wanted to play and about how he could make a little money and about how his friends all had jobs and helped out around their houses and about how maybe he could even save up and buy them a new radio...

His Mother was quiet for a long moment. She looked up at Jon Michael. He was still talking, but she wasn't listening.

"Are you sure this is what you want Jon Michael?" her voice just past a whisper. She asked the question more to the air in the room than to her son.

"Yes Mother." He heard his voice, but couldn't tell whether or not his lips moved.

"All right then," she said turning to face him again for the first time since her first hello. "There are sandwiches on the counter," she added. "Take two and leave one for me. We don't have much time if we are going to get there by seven."

He didn't realize he hadn't told her the time.

There were actually two musician's halls. To go to either, the white or the black one, you went to the same place. In fact, the two buildings were side by side. The route you took to get to either hall was different, however, and although Jon didn't know there were two ways to go, his Mother did.

The white hall was located at 798 W. 28th St., the black hall at 796. To get to the white hall, Jon and his mother took the bus from their apartment, transferred at Central, took another bus to the Claire St. stop, turned right off the bus to 28th and then walked south down 28th the half block to the white musicians' Union Hall.

Had they been going to the black hall, they would have taken the same bus to Central, the same bus after Central, gone past the Claire St. stop, circled back around on to Johnson, got off at Johnson and 26th, walked two blocks along Johnson to 28th, turned north and gone up the other half of the block to the black musicians' hall. This would have added about another half hour to their trip.

They arrived at the white hall about five minutes before seven. The hall was an old closed down shoe store. The large front windows were blocked by heavy red curtains that remained closed, as Fraser would later find out, twenty-four hours a day. As they walked past the storefront windows to the door on the far-right side, Jon turned to the see the words *'AMERICAN FEDERATION OF MUSICIANS LOCAL #9.'* They turned and entered before he could notice the sign on the next window that read in lettering the same size and the same colour, the same gold with black trim, *'AMERICAN FEDERATION OF MUSICIANS LOCAL #535'.*

"Who the hell are you?" A heavy, throaty voice asked. The hell turned into a heck when the voice noticed the woman walk in immediately after Jon Michael. His Mother's mouth started to sound out a word when Jon quickly stepped up. He was much taller than his mother now and when he stood in front of her she disappeared behind him.

"My name is Jon Michael Fraser. I play violin. Mr. Clayton gave me this card." He handed Clayton's business card to the man behind the voice and said, "Mr. Clayton told me to be here at seven o'clock. He said he had a band that he needed me to play with."

"Well, I can see you've got a violin under your arm but you say you're a player?"

The voice couldn't continue. Clayton walked in from one of the small rooms that lined the back and went halfway up the right side of the long narrow room that served as the main hall.

"Fraser, you're late!" it was 6:58. "Hello Gladys." Clayton looked past Fraser to his Mother.

"Hello John," she replied. She ignored Jon's stunned look as he turned to see who the woman was Clayton had called Gladys. It had been a long time since he had heard his Mother's name spoken. So long that he had all but forgotten that she indeed had a name.

"Fraser," he called out again. "You're late. Here's your music." He handed him a black leather folder with the name '*Cherry Hill Social Club*' stenciled on the front.

"You can look this over on the way to the gig. If there is anything you can't play, don't try it, just fake it, just sit up there and wave your arm around like you're making some noise. There's a car waiting out back. Don't get in until they tell you to, don't get out until they tell you to, sit where they tell you to, don't say a word even if they tell you to and whatever you do don't even think about..." He couldn't finish his sentence.

Gladys jumped in. "Excuse Mr. Clayton but how much will the boy be paid?"

"Oh, well, this one is kind of a try out. If Peterson likes him, you know Bill Peterson don't you, the guy from the Deli on 14th?" Gladys nodded. "Peterson's the lead on this gig. If Peterson likes him he will get $1.50 for a weekday gig, $1.85 for a Friday or Saturday night."

Gladys stepped past Fraser. Fraser didn't move. He was still back at 'Gladys.'

"Listen John," she said under her breath, almost too quiet for Jon to hear, but with no shortage of ferocity. "You didn't say nothing about a tryout. You said he was better than any of the other players down here."

34

"Gladys," he replied, his shoulder first dropped then pulled up in a shrug. "This is the way it's done, you know that."

"You get one for free Clayton, that's all. If you don't pay him next time that's it." Her face didn't attempt to hide her anger.

"Don't worry, this is how it works. I won't let anybody screw him over." Clayton stepped past Gladys and said to Jon, "Get moving boy, they're leaving five minutes ago."

Fraser snapped back to life.

He had missed most of what had just gone on. His head had gotten lost in sound that was all around him. As Clayton and Gladys talked Fraser had noticed the small rooms, no bigger than closets, surrounding the main office-type room they had entered into. From each of the small rooms came sounds from unknown, unseen musicians. Scales here, a piece of a song there, a drummer going through a complex set up warm-up rudiments.

Fraser's mind took all these sounds in as one and created a music never before heard. The sum total of all that was going on around him mixed in the ether and funneled down through his ears, in his mouth and nose, through his eyes, his pores. Every opening took in sound. Sound came in from everywhere and somehow made sense once it had traveled up and around his mind for a while.

Clayton's voice had brought Fraser back and he looked at his Mother.

"It's OK dear, go on. Mr. Peterson will see that you get home safely."

"All right Mother," he responded. And as he did, he felt a strange pain swell up in his chest. It entered from the back, just up under his right shoulder blade and quickly swam through him to the front, just right of center, opposite his heart. It settled into a small ball.

Fraser tucked the folder with *'Cherry Hill Social Club'* stenciled on it under the same arm that held his violin and ran tentatively through the hall, the air so thick with sound that he could almost taste it, to a door at the back marked 'EXIT.'

He opened the door and stepped out into the night.

As his foot hit the hard, dirt alley, he was suddenly aware that night had indeed fallen. Of course, night had fallen an hour or so ago. He and his Mother had been on the bus, making their way to Mr. Clayton and the A. F. of M. hall but he hadn't noticed.

As he stepped out into the night, his senses—heightened, electrified by the sounds darting and drifting, swinging and swooning around the hall—suddenly contracted, violently, like a turtle sensing danger and pulling its head back into its shell. His eyes narrowed, partly from stepping from light into dark but more from his attention focusing forward, only forward, to the long black car in front of him.

Every other car was long and black but this car was long... and... black.

"Don't get in until they tell you to, don't get out until they tell you to, sit where they tell you to, don't say a word even if they tell

you to and whatever you do don't even think about . . ." Clayton's words echoed in his mind.

A hand motioned to him. He opened the back door, driver's side and climbed into the car. The car was facing north in the alley behind 28th St. There was not enough room in the alley to turn around. It would have had to come up the alley traveling northward, past the back of the *'AMERICAN FEDERATION OF MUSICIANS LOCAL #535,'* to reach its current location behind the white musician's Union Hall. It would continue north up the alley and out to the rest of the world.

The car was big. Two people in the front, two in the back. He was the third. There was room for several more. His first instinct was to look for the other instruments, see what he was getting himself into. He saw none.

The car jerked a little too roughly as it pulled away from the back of the hall. Fraser looked over his shoulder to see a trailer, half the size of the car in tow behind. The other instruments must be in there, he thought.

"I'm Peterson," a voice from the front called back to him. It sounded like it came from the passenger side. Neither occupant of the front seat turned to face him directly.

"How long you been playing, kid?" The voice was definitely coming from the passenger.

"A few years now," Fraser replied. He could sense all four bodies in the car listening to him.

"A few years huh," Peterson said almost to himself. "Well both Clayton and Redfern say you're pretty good so you should do all right, but you better have a look at that music before we get there. Billy back there is the bass player and if you fuck up he *will* cut your balls off." The body beside Fraser chuckled. Fraser guessed that that was Billy.

He had all but forgotten the violin and folder under his arm. He had carried his violin under his arm for so long now that it felt like a natural extension of his body. The folder didn't add enough of a difference to make it more noticeable. The city lights as they drove provided just enough light for Fraser to get the gist of the music in the black folder with *'Cherry Hill Social Club'* stenciled on it.

The songs were new, but not difficult. Most of his friends at Presidents Memorial High School would have been able to at least make a pretty good attempt at them. There were a few spots that looked a little tricky and room for solos in a few places. He would wait until Peterson asked him if he had any questions before he asked any questions though.

Fraser had no idea where they were, or where they were going. They didn't drive for long. After about twenty minutes, the car turned off the main road and into another alley.

"The *Hill* is just up here," the body next to Fraser leaned over and said.

Fraser snapped upright. He had gotten lost in one of the pieces of sheet music in the folder. It was a tune called *Undecided.* Underneath the title, to the right was the word 'Violin', to the left the names of the composers: Shavers & Robin. The notation was beautiful. The notes danced on the lines and spaces. He could hear the song as he looked at the paper. This had never happened with the stuff Mr. Redfern gave them at school. He was lost in this one before he had played even the first note.

The car pulled to a stop and was shoved forward an extra half foot or so by the trailer behind. Three doors flew open. Fraser opened his door a half second later. The alley he stepped into looked like the alley behind the Union Hall where they had started. But this was clearly not the same place.

Peterson headed for a door. The building was low, concrete, the only entrance or opening of any kind (at least in the back) was the door Peterson and the other body from the front seat had just gone through. The word E-N-T-R-A-N-C-E was painted in faded yellow above the door. After that word (musicians) appeared in smaller, black lettering, not as faded. Fraser stepped to follow Peterson.

"Hey, littleshit," a voice from behind him called out. The sound came from over by the trailer.

"Where do you think you're going? Get your ass back here and carry this shit in."

Fraser did as he was told. The other two from the back seat carried the contents of the trailer through the entrance into a small area just inside the door. The body that had been sitting beside him told him not to go any further in until Peterson told them it was all right.

It took about fifteen minutes to empty the contents of the trailer. By the time they had finished Peterson and the other front seat body hadn't returned.

"Wait here," the body, which must have been Billy said and leaned up against the wall beside the entrance.

Fraser waited, leaning up against the same wall. He stood to Billy's right so that Billy was between him and the door.

"Peterson said this was your first time?" Billy's voice rose at the end turning it into a question.

"Yea," was all Fraser could reply.

"Well, we'll go easy on ya," Billy chuckled again, the same chuckle from the car.

Another twenty minutes passed before the car's driver emerged from the entrance and said, "O. k., everything's set up, let's go."

"You in tune kid?" Billy turned and said to Fraser as he leaned forward, up from the wall and started into the building.

"No, I mean I don't know." Fraser remembered tuning before he put his violin in its case before he left home but that seemed like years ago now, he was sure it would be of tune by now. "Ah, yea, I think so."

"You better do more than 'think so' kid. Our first tune is on the stand *right now*. Peterson is calling it out and introducing us *right now*. We're walking on that stage and starting. This is no fucking rehearsal!" Billy's voice got more and more intense as his words poured out.

"Yea, I'm OK," Fraser felt lightheaded. He could begin to taste the sandwiches from the kitchen counter in the back of his throat.

"You had better be OK," Billy said. "Peterson may have been joking, but I *will* cut your balls off if you make me look like a fucking idiot, you dig?"

Billy led Fraser through a narrow couple of hallways, up a short flight of stairs to a door. "This is it boy, everyone else is already out there. We step on last, sit down and we're off ok?" Billy asked the question but didn't wait for a reply. He swung the door open, grabbed Fraser by the arm and pulled him through.

Fraser had been outside for nearly an hour. The hallway leading to the stage door was dark. His eyes had grown totally accustomed to the dark. As he was pulled through the door, his eyes shut tightly, his hand went up to his face as an incredibly bright light flooded over him.

The next thing he heard was laughter. Not a lot of laughter. Just a couple of people. Something was wrong. More laughter, he heard Billy now, right beside him, screaming, out of control, he thought he heard him fall over.

Fraser turned his head to the floor, shading himself, slowly opened his eyes and looked up. The first thing he noticed was all their stuff, still in cases in the middle of a small bandstand. Then he saw Billy (for the first time in full light) doubled over, laughing uncontrollably. Then he turned to see the other three bodies from the car in similar states in front of the bandstand. There was nobody else. Just a dozen empty tables scattered around a small dance floor.

"You should have seen the look on your face kid," Billy screamed. "I thought you were gonna piss your pants." The laughter only got louder.

Peterson stepped up. "All right, boys, fun's over let's get to work. We only have a half hour to get ready before they open the doors. People are starting to show up already."

SECOND SET

I. "Mom?" It was a question. He knew she would be awake. He turned it into a question as he walked through the door.

"Yes baby, I'm in here." She was sitting on the couch, radio turned all the way down, dial still glowing soft orange.

She was exactly where he knew she would be, sitting exactly the way he knew she would be sitting, doing exactly what he knew she would be doing. For her part, she was ready for every move he made as well. It was if they had rehearsed this moment many times before.

"They really liked me."

"I knew they would, my love."

"Mr. Peterson even paid me. Everybody said that he never pays anyone on their first night."

"That's great baby."

"Mr. Peterson said that I could play with him on Thursday and Saturday nights. If it's alright with you that is?"

"What about your schoolwork?"

"School's not hard. Besides, I can make some money. Lots of my friends have already dropped out of school and are working full-time."

"No son of mine is dropping out of school. I don't care how much money you can make."

"I never said I would drop out of school. I just said that lots of other people are."

"I never said you would drop out, baby. Now, come over here, sit down with me. Let your Mother hold you like she used to. I'll turn up the radio."

"Aw, Mom, I'm too big for that now."

"Nonsense, come here."

He put down the case with his violin inside and laid the black music folder beside it. His Mother shifted to her left making room for him on the couch. He sank into the couch, letting himself slide down, almost off the edge, getting his head down low enough to rest it on her shoulder. She turned up the radio.

W.B.E.Z. had changed in the years since they first moved into the apartment at the corner of 12th and Cottonwood. At first, the station went to static by 11:00 pm. Now, it was broadcasting around the clock. At this hour of the morning it broadcast mostly ballads, slower show tunes. The disc jockeys could even slip in a little Coleman Hawkins or Lester Young so long as they were slower numbers, more familiar stuff.

"I like the saxophone," he said. "It's got a great sound. That guy can almost make it sound like a woman crying." He was looking out into the sound. His mother was staring into the same spot.

"I don't know baby," she replied. "I'm not a fan, it's really not that versatile."

They were quiet for a long time.

"Do you want me to tell you another story about your Daddy?" she asked.

They were quiet for a long time.

"No Mom. I just want to listen."

A female singer came on, an old song. Fraser had played it two hours earlier at *Cherry Hill*. Peterson had counted it in fast. Fraser could hardly keep up. The version coming out of the radio now was slow. It sounded like an elegy: *"Pack up all your cares and woe..."*

"I have to go to bed Mother."

"I know baby. I'm going to sleep out here with the radio tonight."

He got up, picked up his violin and music, went into his room and closed his door. She lay down on the couch and closed her eyes.

The conversation was coming. He played it out in his head as he lay down in his bed.

"I have to go Mother," he rehearsed silently.

"I know baby," he heard his Mother's reply. "It will break my heart." It was as if they were actually having the conversation. Perhaps they were; him in his room, her a door away.

"You know I have to break your heart Mother. There is no other way."

He thought he heard a faint sob from the other room. He got up and slowly opened his bedroom door. His Mother was sound asleep, breathing slowly. Her chest moving up and down, in then out.

He went back to bed and closed his eyes. His mind didn't race. It drifted slowly, like his Mother's breath.

As he lay in bed his mind wandered and he saw things. Things he hadn't seen before. People, places, women, music. For the first time he could remember, he could only see things, there was no sound. The music was there, but it was silent.

Without realizing it he slipped into a dream. He dreamt he was in a big parade. Marching bands, floats, clowns, acrobats on stilts waving flags of every colour he could imagine. He was in the middle of all this. Just him. No instrument, no flag. He didn't belong to any group or any collection of people marching, yet he was in the procession.

Suddenly, he veered away from the march and walked down a narrow side street. In the dream, he was suddenly aware that a group of marchers had also broken away from the main group and were following him. They followed him to a small grassy field. He climbed on top a narrow embankment, turned and faced his followers. He started to speak and the group that had followed him fell quiet, as if waiting for some divine message. In an instant, his perception changed and he was floating above the crowd watching the congregation from above. He could see himself talking to the gathered group but he couldn't hear what his dream-self was saying. The crowd hung on his every word. They were listening to him. Ready to follow.

II. They really did like him.

Peterson liked his playing. The crowds liked him too. Before long, Peterson had him working most nights of the week, except Sunday. His Mother wouldn't let him play on Sunday. There was no particular reason. They never went to any church. "I don't like all those boring hymns," Mother would say. There was plenty of work to be had on Sundays as well. In fact, there was an open house and dance at the Union Hall that Fraser would have fit right into, but Mother still said it wasn't right to play on Sunday. At first Fraser argued with her about Sundays but quickly gave up. In truth, he enjoyed the time off.

Fraser came home from his first gig at *Cherry Hill* in love, first love. Mr. Redfern at Presidents Memorial had started the fire. He gave Fraser a peek, a taste, a glimpse through a window at what music could be. Clayton sent him to Peterson, and Peterson gave him his first kiss.

For that first few weeks he was in love. Then it started to change. Just little bits, here and there. He would start to look around while he was playing then punish himself when he realized his attention was wandering. He began to ask Peterson for solos. At first, he had been content to take solos only when Peterson had told him to.

He began to notice other peoples' mistakes: late entries here, someone too loud or too quiet over there, the drummer or bass player holding the rest of the band back or pushing them too far ahead. Just little things but within about six months or so, the love had turned to like, then to something he didn't really have a name for.

His relationship with Mother changed in exactly the same way. A minute later getting home one day, a couple more the next. Getting home and going straight to bed, not staying up to tell her how his day had been. On Sundays, he started sleeping later and later. Sometimes he would even stay in his room after he had woken and just lay in bed. He could hear his Mother moving around, cleaning, making breakfast. He could hear the radio but he didn't want to be a part of it anymore.

Soon his schoolwork began to suffer.

One day, his assignments not done, he got on the bus and headed down to the Union Hall. The idea of truancy had never crossed his mind before. It still hadn't, this wasn't a conscious decision, he just took a right instead of a left. He knew as the bus pulled up to the Claire St. stop that he would never go back to school again. He was sixteen (almost seventeen).

The Union Hall became his school and his home. As he walked through the door that day, no one gave him a second glance. It was as if this too had been rehearsed, a ready-made plan that was just coming to fruition.

"Hey Fraser, you want to work tonight?" It was Clayton. "I've got a gig out at 33rd and Oak, it's an old folks home. They want to hear all that old stuff, you know, relive their youth." Clayton was chuckling, amused with himself.

"Yea, sure," Fraser replied. "What time is Peterson picking me up?"

"No Peterson this time kid, he can't make it, you're the boss." Clayton spoke with absolutely no additional emotion whatsoever. It was as if he had just told Fraser the score of a ball game no one really cared about.

And just like that Fraser became a leader. Being the leader meant more responsibility. He had to introduce the band, call out the numbers, handle the money (turn it over to Clayton mostly) and make sure everything ran smoothly on the job. All this seemed like such a natural fit to Fraser that no one even questioned him when they showed up and he was running the show.

He still worked for Peterson and a few of the other guys who ran bands through the Hall but now he was truly one of them. This not only had its privileges, but its responsibilities as well. The most important thing was *being* at the Hall. There were rooms to practice. Larger rooms to work with sections and small groups and the main room could be booked for large group rehearsals. All this gave an air of seriousness and respectability, especially during the day when the social clubs would send their entertainment coordinators or event arrangers or sometimes even their social managers down to book an act.

Mother didn't question Fraser about school.

Before he dropped out, he would leave in the morning, go to the hall after school and get home around 6:00 if there wasn't a job for him, around midnight if there was. Now, he was gone about the same amount of time and although someone from the school must have come by to see where Fraser was, his Mother never questioned him about it, despite her earlier warnings.

The daily workings, the rooms, and the insides of the hall opened up to Fraser. His newfound position also opened up the back of the hall, outside, in the alley.

The first few times Fraser had stepped out into the alley he hadn't even noticed the various bodies spread out around the back of the building. A couple over there talking, one or two in a doorway smoking, another one over there taking a drink from a small bottle. As time wore on, he began slowly to be aware of this other world, back behind the two Musicians' Union Halls that sat beside each other.

From the front, they looked like two separate buildings but from the back you couldn't tell one from the other. They both shared the same back wall. In the darkness of the back alley, peoples' faces tended to meld together, you couldn't distinguish features too well. It was a dark, almost mysterious place. It wasn't the real world.

"Hey man, you got an extra smoke?" a voice from behind Fraser asked. He and Peterson were taking a break, hanging out behind the Hall, out for a cigarette and some fresh air.

"Uh, yea, just a minute." Fraser fumbled through his pockets. He turned and placed the cigarette in the longest, blackest fingers he had ever seen.

"Hey Peters," the voice said, looking past Fraser.

"Hey James, any work lately?" Peterson asked nonchalantly.

"Shit, no man, it's all boring shit anyway man, I wouldn't take it if it was there to take."

"I hear that man," Peterson replied.

He and Fraser returned to the inside of the hall.

"Who was that?" Fraser was startled for the first time in a long time.

"That was James Johnson. The best bass player around here, shit, probably the best player around anywhere. They say he used to play with Buddy Bolden, before Bolden ended up in the nut-house."

"Who's Buddy Bolden?" Fraser truly did not know.

"Buddy Bolden?" Peterson was incredulous. "I keep forgetting you're just a kid. Man, you better start asking some questions around this place if you're ever going to figure all this stuff out."

That was the last, and the best, advice Peterson ever gave Jon Michael Fraser.

III. Eventually even the music began to bore him. The music Peterson played, and the music he had to play at the gigs Clayton set up for him lost its lustre. It got old. The gigs were social gigs. Gigs where people wanted to hear all their favourite songs. Fraser grew tired of the notes on the page. He asked Peterson for more solos and Peterson gave them to him, but before long even the solos all started to sound the same.

Fraser's boredom wasn't picked up by his audiences. None of the other players in his groups sensed anything was wrong either. Fraser had had a meteoric ride to the top of the social club scene and stayed there, but his playing became automatic. He knew what got a rise out of the crowd and what would go by unnoticed.

He used to play a little game. He would play a solo in one song. Really go for it, stretch out a little, maybe slide around a few wrong notes, get peoples' attention. The next song or maybe a couple of songs later, he would play exactly the same solo, note for note, same mistakes and all. After the set, he would ask guys in the band and some people in the audience which solo they liked better. Every single time, every person he would ask would have a preference for one or the other. Most people had good evidence to support their choice for either solo A or the other solo A. Fraser would listen carefully, make up stories about why he did this here and that there. While he was thinking "you stupid bastards," the smile on his face and the pleasant nodding never gave him away.

It was the music on the page that became boring. Fraser just started to hear more. He couldn't yet articulate what was happening inside him, but he was beginning to notice the gaps. Gaps between the notes.

The social club gigs needed to stay on the written page. The dancers, the old folks needed to know what was coming next. They needed to know when the song was ending, when it was going to the bridge, when the next surprise was coming. But Fraser began to feel the gaps, the space between the notes on the page and the potential that lay within the notes. Play a ballad as fast as possible. Play a fast song slow. Take the written notes as the jumping off point and see what other stories they could tell.

Those around him had no interest in any of these other stories. It wasn't their fault. They just didn't have spaces that needed filling.

Fraser also began spending a lot less time at home.

"When will you be home dear?" Mother asked.

Fraser stopped in the doorway. "I don't know. Clayton wants me to stop by the hall after the gig again and drop off the money. I may hang around for a while and look at some new charts."

"Ok, dear, I'll wait up, maybe we can talk again, ok?"

It wasn't ok and they would not talk. Fraser had gotten into the habit of checking to see if the light in her bedroom was on before he went up the stairs to the apartment. If it was on, she would be awake. If it was on, he would wander around the neighbourhood until it went off and then he would go up to bed himself. If he stayed out all night, it wouldn't make a difference. When he woke up, he would just head down the Hall anyway. He hardly even ate at home anymore.

He began spending more and more time behind the two Halls, the alley behind *AMERICAN FEDERATION OF MUSICIANS #9* and *#535*. Since their first impromptu meeting, he was out there to be with only one person. Something drew Fraser to him. Something subtler than gravity. It may have been his voice, rich, gravelly, alive. It may have been his demeanour, so smooth it was as if he would be cool to the touch. It may have been his hands with the longest, blackest fingers Fraser had ever seen. More than likely, it was the sense Fraser had that just below the surface of this man lay fire waiting to get out, a snake, ready to strike. Not the kind of snake that would dart at you, sink its fangs in and kill you with its poison. The kind of snake that would slowly wind its way around you while you were busy doing something else and then gradually squeeze your life away without you knowing what was going on, until it was too late.

James Johnson used to spend a lot of time out in the alley. By this time, J. J.'s better days were behind him. He lived long on legend though. It was said that J. J. was Buddy Bolden's bass player. Fraser quickly found out that Buddy Bolden was a trumpet player from New Orleans who, as legend had it, could play so loud and strong that he once caused a woman to go into labour just by passing by her house during a Mardi Gras parade. The women that told him this story in the alley said that "that little woman's baby heard Bolden's horn, thought it was the Trumpets of Jericho themselves and had to get right on out and see for himself what going on."

Of course, Bolden ended up going mad and died in an insane asylum, adding greatly to J. J.'s mystique. Someone else had told Fraser that J. J.'s playing was the thing that made Bolden snap. "J. J. can fuck with your mind, boy. That motherfucker can play that bass and get his notes all up inside your head and make you see shit you ain't never seen."

Fraser had found a new love.

He began to spend all the time he was at the hall out back waiting for Johnson.

"How you doing boy?"

"Not bad Mr. Johnson, how are you today?"

"Shit boy if you don't call me J. J., I'm gonna bust your ass. You don't need to play that shit back here."

"Do you want a smoke?" J. J. never had his own smokes. Fraser really didn't smoke, but he got in the habit of carrying a pack around in case he needed to buy a minute of someone else's time.

"Ya, that would be nice. What did you say your name was kid?"

"Fraser, my first name is Jon but everybody calls me Fraser."

"Jon Fraser huh, and what do you play Jon Fraser?"

"I play violin."

"You play what?" Johnson stepped back, true disbelief crossed his face. "You play violin? Show me your fingers boy, you can't be no violin player."

Fraser held out his hands. J. J. grabbed by the wrist and pulled him closer.

"Shit boy, look at your goddamn hands, your fingers are way too long for the violin. How can you move around on that skinny little shit instrument? Your hands could wrap themselves twice around the neck of that thing."

Fraser hadn't thought about it, but Johnson was right. His hands were huge. Fraser had always thought that this was what made it so easy for him to work his way around his instrument.

"I'm a great player, everybody likes my playing, there's nothing I can't play!" Fraser had forgotten his modesty.

"Nothing you can't play huh?" Johnson leaned into him.

Fraser leaned in the other direction.

"All right. Wait here. I'm going to go inside, get us a little room." A wide smile crept across Johnson's face. "I'll clear out some space where we won't be disturbed, then I'll come out and get you. When we go inside, keep your head down and stay close behind me."

Johnson disappeared inside the *AMERICAN FEDERATION OF MUSICIANS LOCAL #535*. Fraser was frozen to the spot where J. J. had left him. Ten minutes later Johnson came out and said, "OK boy, now follow me and stay close, it's cool out here but if some of those guys in there catch you, they'll kill at least or worse you and trust me you want none of that."

Fraser was too excited to hear the threat, he wouldn't have bought it even if he had.

IV. Fraser stepped through the door. He recognized the situation. He had been here before. Once again, he lost all sense of the peripheral and could only focus on the spot directly in front of him. This time the spot was the small patch of dark skin between the bottom of Johnson's hairline and top of his collar. The white rim of the shirt collar would have stood out, in sharp contrast to the dark brown skin if not for a slight yellowing which acted like a buffer between the dark and the light.

Fraser followed the patch of skin through the back door of *AMERICAN FEDERATION OF MUSICIANS LOCAL #535,* turned immediately to the right, went through another door (J. J. turned quickly and told Fraser to shut the door as soon as the two were through) and down a short flight of stairs. The room smelled of wood and oils, mixed with a sharp, mildly unpleasant, sort of turpentine smell.

"OK boy, we're here," Johnson stopped suddenly. Fraser almost walked into him. "Now, find yourself a violin and let's go."

Fraser looked around. They were in a workshop. Obviously, an instrument repair shop. There was a guitar in need of strings, a couple of trumpets apparently in good order, a few more in pieces, a saxophone, a couple of clarinets, other miscellaneous instruments stood in various stages of both dis- and re- pair. On a small workbench along the near side wall were two violins. Fraser picked up the first. It had fresh strings, the action was fast and well balanced it was ready to go. He picked up the other. The second one was at the other end of the repair process; very playable but in need of a tune-up. Fraser's inclination was to use the first violin, but then he thought that whoever had fixed it up would notice the littlest bit of fresh sweat on the clean fingerboard. He decided to play it safe and use the second. No one would notice a little extra use on that one.

"You ready, boy?" Fraser turned again to see Johnson standing before him with a well-aged, full-sized bass nestling effortlessly into Johnson's chest. The standard among the bands he had played with was to use three-quarter size basses. Fraser had always thought they were big. This bass was huge. It stood as high as he did. The tip of the headstock was several inches taller than Johnson. The neck met the body about mid chest on Johnson.

As huge as the instrument was, in an instant Fraser's eyes grew accustomed to it and the bass seemed to meld with Johnson. J. J. held it at such an angle that he seemed to be cradling it, holding it close, like a crying lover or a hurt child. The bass and Johnson made a union Fraser had never seen before, not with any other musician, not with any two other people.

"What are we going to play?" Fraser asked.

"Well you said you could play anything, let's play anything."

"Ya, but where's the music?" Fraser was waiting for the music.

"Here it is boy, try to keep up." Johnson started.

It was a heartbeat. A slow steady pulse. 1 . . . 2 . . . 3 . . . 4 and again 1 . . . 2 . . . 3 . . . 4. The air changed. The walls disappeared. The smell and the dust and the light and the dark left. The air became tangible. Like a thick fog, but dry, no moisture. All Fraser could see was Blue. The blue right where the sky changes from blue to black as your eyes travel from the horizon up to the heavens. That exact point. That's where Johnson was, right at that blue.

That's where he stayed too. Fraser had no idea for how long. Then the 1 . . . 2 . . . . 3 . . . 4 evolved into 1 . . . 2 . . . 3 . . . 4 & a. That was Fraser's cue.

He picked up the violin, raised the bow and drew it down across the strings, long and slow. His notes were rays of sunshine. Every note a bright light, calling down, darting around the blue even though the tempo was almost a dirge.

But rays of sunshine have no place in that moment between darkness and light. They belong to another world and Fraser knew it.

J. J. continued. His playing went deeper into the night. It went out to the street, into the alley behind the Union Halls, to the coffee bars and the nightclubs, back to the Hall for a late-night jam session, into the bedrooms of the one night stands and the other lovers, to the cigarettes Fraser had for him, through the back door of the *AMERICAN FEDERATION OF MUSICIANS LOCAL #535*, down the stairs and right back to where it had started.

Fraser's playing stayed at the *Cherry Hill Social Club*.

"I want that," Fraser stared into the smile as it grew across James Johnson's face.

"Hm, you want what, boy?"

"I want what you just did."

"You ain't never gonna get it on that thing."

Fraser looked down at the violin in his hand, "This? This isn't mine. I'll go next door and get my own instrument, then I can do it."

"No," Johnson replied, "It's not the instrument, it's you. Any fool could take one look at you and know you are no violin player. Shit boy, look at yourself. You're taller than me and your goddamn hands look like you got baseball mitts on. Shit boy, you're a bass player. Let some other fool have the violin, it's not for you. The only thing you can play is this."

With that Johnson tilted the bass away from his own body and towards Fraser's. Fraser placed the violin and bow back on the bench he had gotten them from, stretched out his hand and took hold of the bass as it fell from Johnson's left hand to his.

"Are you sure I can play your instrument?" Fraser asked.

"Shit no, you *can not* play my instrument. My instrument is upstairs, I don't know whose fucking instrument this is. Play my instrument, shit," J. J. continued under his breath.

Fraser let the bass fall into his chest as he had seen Johnson do just a minute ago. The wood was still warm. The headstock brushed against Fraser's ear, pushing his hair aside as it moved. He felt the curves of the instrument press into his chest, his hip, his thigh, as gravity pulled it closer to him. He accepted the weight. The bass was perfectly balanced. He was the force standing between the instrument remaining upright and falling to the ground. His left hand reached up toward the headstock, stopping at the end of the neck and reaching around. His fingers spread out. He could feel the air between his left hand's fingers. Never before had he noticed this. His middle finger pressed into the second thickest string about three inches from the top. His right hand came from the other side and reached out to the middle of the body, where the strings are suspended in mid-air, past the fingerboard, above the body, between the two holes in the shape of 'f's. His first finger, bent almost parallel to the strings, touched the same second thickest string that his left hand was touching a couple of feet away. His right fingers pressed against the string, moving it ever so slightly against the air. His left fingers pressed into the string, holding it against the neck. He could feel the string digging in into his flesh, just to the point before pleasure could be mistaken for pain, on both hands. As he let out his breath, his right hand released and set the second thickest string to life.

Fraser had never felt anything like it before. The instrument vibrated, resonated, setting the air in motion, his body in motion, the whole world in motion.

"See boy, I told you, you play bass."

V. James Johnson taught Jon Michael Fraser everything there was to know in that instant in the basement of the black musicians' Union Hall. Both of them knew it but at Fraser's insistence, Johnson agreed to more formally teach the young player the instrument. Never again would Fraser play the violin. The bass player was born.

"First rule, if you don't hear nothing, don't play nothing." Johnson liked being the teacher. He presented his tutelage like a Sunday morning preacher. Whether or not the fire and brimstone was intentional, Fraser heard it and Johnson probably did mean it that way.

The two would meet at Johnson's place. Johnson had a small apartment in the basement of *Old Mrs. Robinson's Rooming House. Mrs. Robinson's* was famous in most parts of town, but Fraser had never heard of it. Twenty or so years ago it was the most famous brothel in the area. When the first Mrs. Robinson died, her daughter inherited the house. Shortly after taking over the family industry the second Mrs. Robinson found Jesus and quickly decided that her Born Again values differed too greatly from her mother's more liberal mindset to continue the business as it had previously been run.

Coincidentally, that was about the same time the white folks stopped coming by *Old Mrs. Robinson's* and probably explains why Fraser was unaware of the house until his lesson with J. J.

Johnson took the room in the basement because it was quiet and more or less safe. A fair bit of sunlight came into the room. There were several windows above ground level that followed the sun across the sky regardless of the season. The windows were small enough that they were easily blacked out though, turning day into night if need be. The street had little traffic, especially during the day and J. J. could sleep. He was rarely there in the evenings.

Their lessons constituted of three parts. First, scales. Up and down. Root to the ninth.

"Any dumb fuck can go from root to root," Johnson took on his preacher voice again. "It takes a real man to go to the ninth. Listen to it," he ordered, "you just resolve it, just make it sound pretty again and then BAM, you slip past it, teasing them a bit. It's like a woman, leaning over just far enough to let you see that she's got something under that shirt then standing up before you have the chance to get a real good look."

Fraser promised himself to look down more girl's tops.

"Don't think of them like scales," J. J. would continue, "think of them like chords. Follow all your chords from the root to the ninth then back down. When some asshole calls out some chord changes, you got to see your neck in all different ways, different for each chord."

Second, was songs.

"Shit, you only need to know two songs."

"What do you mean man, there are thousands of songs?"

"What did I tell you about talking back to me?" Johnson had told him to shut up and listen. Fraser had forgot.

Johnson's face would scowl and he would say something like, "If you don't shut the fuck up and follow directions you can get the fuck out of here. I don't have time to waste on this shit." But on the inside, he would be smiling. There was once again a finely choreographed routine between young man and old. They both knew their parts and played them perfectly.

"Do you want to know or not?"

"Yea, shit man, I'm sorry."

"SHIT?! Don't you ever swear in my motherfucking house! Didn't your mother teach you any goddamn fucking manners? Shit."

Fraser had wished Johnson had left his Mother out of this. "Yea, oh man, I'm sorry, show me, please."

"Shit . . .," J. J. was still recovering.

J. J. stammered out this next part, "Play the blues for those who can hear it and those, goddamn, *I Got Rhythm* changes for those who can't. Now get out of here, you've upset far too much already today."

The third part, when they got around to it, was just playing. The piano that used to sit in the parlour of *Old Mrs. Robinson's* was moved downstairs and sat in J. J.'s room. Johnson could handle his own on it and would play the chords for Fraser while he navigated his way around this instrument that quickly felt as natural to him as waking up, putting his left leg down the left side of his pants, the right down the other, pulling them up and getting on with his day.

By this point, getting on with Fraser's day had less and less to do with *American Federation of Musicians Union Local #9*. It had almost nothing to do with his Mother.

It wasn't to the point where Fraser would be allowed through the front door of Hall #535, but Johnson had arranged to let him stand by the back door. The back door was often left open to let the fresh air in. Fraser would stand there transfixed.

After most of the gigs around town were done, Hall #9 would quiet down. Sometimes, someone would stop by and sweep up. Sometimes, a member who was too drunk to go home or had tried to go home and been unceremoniously sent away, would be around, sleeping in a practice room. Sometimes a girl would be brought back for a little 'quiet conversation.' But, for the most part, once the gig was over, so was Hall #9.

Hall #535 was very much the opposite. After the paying work was done, the real music began. Pretty well every musician would come back and the party would continue until at least dawn. It wasn't just a party though. This was the place where the young players would cut their teeth. The place where the old players would show why they were the old players.

Before long, Fraser could identify the different players by their sound alone. Not by the style each person used or the instrument they played, but more by the depth and nuances or lack thereof in their tone. Johnson had told him once, you could figure out who *any* musician was whether they were playing their main instrument or not just by listening to the phrasing and the attitude they put into the notes. Fraser put this theory to the test and proved it right every night at the back door of Hall #535.

Fraser would make up stories about the sounds he heard coming through the doorway. Stories about the sounds and the people making them. This one beat his wife, this one had no wife, this one thinks the whole world is out to get him, the whole world actually is out to get this one. They were all there. He was all there as well.

There were many voices that drew Fraser to that back door those nights, but there was only one that kept him coming back.

VI. "Hey, are you J. J.'s boy?" The door flew open, almost catching Fraser in the face as his mind was drifting away.

"Are you Johnson's boy?!" the man repeated. He stood in front of Fraser with a look of panic on his face.

"What do mean?" Fraser stammered.

"Are you or are you not the white boy that's been hanging around with J. J. busting his ass, bugging him to teach you that bass?"

Fraser figured that could only be him and replied "Yea, I guess that's me."

"Well then get on in here boy, we've got ourselves an emergency."

The man who had flung the door open almost catching Fraser in the face turned and went back through the door with just as much veracity as before. After a second he stuck his head back out the door and said to a stunned Fraser, "You coming or not?"

Fraser's mind was racing. Was something wrong with J. J.? What the hell are these guys gonna do to me? I can't go in there?! These thoughts and more twisted through Fraser's head as he followed the stranger in and through the door.

"This way," the guy leading instructed.

They went past the door which lead to the basement, the one Fraser had gone down before, past a few more doors, closed, leading to other places he hadn't been and down a short narrow hallway, ending up in front of yet another door.

"He's in there and it's not pretty," Fraser's tour guide spoke as he opened the door.

There was James Johnson, bass face down on the floor, his body slumped back in a chair, a mass against the back wall of the small, closet-sized room. The chair which held up his body seemed precariously perched, as if it would fall over, sending him crashing down into his bass if the balance was disturbed even the slightest bit.

"Oh, God," Fraser managed.

"No shit," said the man who had lead him this far.

"Is he dead?" Fraser asked, both men's eyes fixed on the mass in front of them.

"No," the man chuckled. "He just got an earlier start than usual tonight. Usually, he makes it to the end of the night before he ends up like this."

"What do you mean? J. J. doesn't do shit like this." Fraser's voice sounded like a child's and he knew it. Even as he spoke the words, he felt like he had been lied to yet again.

"This old junkie," the man laughed again. "Shit boy, maybe not in the daytime when you're hanging around his place, but in here, well, you're looking at it."

The two were quiet for a moment or two. Then the first man spoke.

"Here's the deal boy. Our friend here is the only bass player in the house tonight. J. J. keeps on bragging about how you're the baddest player he's ever seen. Now is your chance to prove it."

"You mean you want me to sit in? In there? Now?" Fraser pointed over his left shoulder, noise from what seemed like a large, or if not large then at least boisterous, crowd came through the wall behind them.

"It's either that, or we don't play and that wouldn't go over too well with the locals if you know what I mean."

Fraser didn't know what he meant but he didn't belabour the point either. "I don't think so man. J. J. told me that I wasn't supposed to even be in here."

"Well there ain't a lot old J. J. can do about it now, is there?" There wasn't.

"But I'm white." This was the first time Fraser had ever uttered those words.

"Shit boy, that don't matter anymore. Nobody cares. Shit if Charlie Christian can play with Benny Goodman, whose gonna care whether you're white, black, purple or green. If you can play as well as J. J. says you can, nobody will care what colour you are. If you play the way Johnson brags you do, you could even be a woman and no one would give a shit. Come on, let's go."

The man stepped into the room with Johnson and his bass. Leaning forward, he picked up the instrument, brushing up against Johnson's chair. The chair did not topple over. Rather, it fell forward, landing on all four legs, propping Johnson into more upright position than before.

"Give me a hand," the he said.

He handed the bass to Fraser and pushed the chair, and J. J., further into the corner so neither would fall over. He then stepped out of the room, closed the door, turned to Fraser and said, "Don't worry kid, just keep your head down, and play. We'll tuck you way at the back of the stage. No one will hardly be able to even see you. Anyways, nobody watches the band. They're just musicians, you don't need to watch them to make them work."

"Follow me." The man who had led Fraser this far took him further into the hall. As they walked on, the noise from the invisible crowd grew louder and louder. When they were back with J. J., the crowd seemed to be just behind a wall. Now, the noise seemed to be coming from all around, engulfing them.

Fraser's guide led him to yet another door, turned and said, "Alright, the band is on the other side of this door. I'll go through first, just turn to the right and pull up close to the drums. The guys are expecting you, no one else should be paying too much attention to what's going on."

"What are we playing?"

"Just what J. J. taught you to play. Don't worry boy it'll be alright."

Fraser stepped through the door. He carried J. J.'s bass in front of himself, hiding himself from the crowd or maybe the crowd from him. Immediately, turning to the right, Fraser found the drums and moved up close beside. Once the bass was in place, he looked up.

Three pairs of eyes were fixed on him: drums, tenor sax and piano player's. Beyond them, a thick dark curtain filtered out most of the noise that was building behind.

From the other side of the curtain Fraser could hear the voice of the man who had brought him into the hall, onto the stage.

"Ok, ok, calm down, we shall get underway. LADIES AND GENTLEMEN, PLEASE WELCOME, THE FINEST BAND THIS SIDE OF THE HOUR, THE LOCAL #535 *ALL-STARS*!!!"

With that the curtain opened. The three pairs of eyes on stage that didn't belong to Fraser were still staring at him. Fraser's eyes were firmly fixed on the ground. With a tentative 1 . . . 2 . . . 3 . . . 4 the drummer counted them in.

By beat 3 and 1/2 Fraser realized he had no idea what key they were playing in or for that matter, what song they were playing.

Before panic could even present itself as an option, James Johnson's words came back to him: "Play the blues for those who can hear it and those goddamn, *'I Got Rhythm'* changes for those who can't."

Fraser guessed that this was a blues crowd. By beat four he had guessed that this would be in the key of b-flat, a horn's key. On a solid down beat, beat one, Fraser was in. In with a glorious, rich, low b-flat that shook the very floor of the hall, sending vibrations up into the legs of the tables, chairs and people, setting everything attached to those legs into motion as well.

He was moving, slow, swirling around, a steady 1 . . . 2 . . . 3 . . . 4 & a. The rest of the band joined in one by one. Piano first, then tenor and finally trumpet. Trumpet. The man who had brought him into this place and shown him J. J. and gotten him onto the stage was playing the trumpet. Fraser would register the surprise later.

This was a slow blues. Deep and slow. Fraser went with it. Back to his Mother's lap listening to Jack Teagarden, to Mr. Redfern's band room, to Clayton and the AFofM (#9), to Peterson and Gladys, to his first gig, to the violin, to his father. To his father, Fraser was stuck there for a moment or two, he went on to J. J. and the Blue in the basement (probably directly below where he was standing right now), to the alley, to the door, to J. J. semi-conscious in a practice room just a few feet away.

After he had been to all those places, he went further. He went out into the night searching for the Blue right where the sky changes from blue to black as you follow it from the horizon up to the heavens. Fraser could see the ground. He could see the sky. He took one step closer, but the Blue didn't get any nearer. He took another step, but the Blue seemed to be further away.

And just as suddenly as it had started, it was over. The band ended and he was back.

Applause, loud applause. The night was over. Fraser had no idea how long they had been playing. Slowly he began to notice sweat, a lot of sweat, pouring down his face, drenching his shirt. A blister was forming on the index finger of his right hand. His left hand had serious grooves dug into each finger. As he began to accept the sweat, the pain began in earnest in both his hands.

Fraser looked at his hands while so many people swarmed around him. With a start, he looked up. He was searching for only one face. So many faces, but J. J.'s was missing.

VII. "Where's J. J.?" Fraser asked the only face he recognized, the face that began this night's adventure.

"Shit, he's alright, probably just coming around. He's gonna be pissed he missed this. Shit boy, you had them right where you wanted them. Shit if you weren't so white, I bet you'd be beating off all those ladies with a stick right about now."

Fraser didn't care. He hadn't noticed any ladies and he didn't care. His mind was on J. J.

He put the bass down and cut through the crowd, back to the room where the two had left Johnson. Hours must have past since they left the old bass player passed out in the closet-sized practice room. The door was open. The light inside the room was on. Fraser could sense motion coming from inside.

"Shit boy," Johnson's words were slow, slurred, but deliberate. "I knew that was you from the instant before you played your first note. It was like the air got greedy, waiting for you to start. I could taste the anticipation as it waited for you to fill it up."

"Are you alright?" The last thing on Fraser's mind was the air. Except to ensure that air continued to flow in and out of James Johnson's lungs.

"Ah, shit boy, of course I'm alright, just got a little bit carried away that's all. Now get your ass back to that stage, get my bass, bring it back here and give me a hand getting home. My legs ain't as sturdy as they used to be.

74

Johnson wasn't joking. In fact his legs were significantly more than a little unsteady. As he and Fraser stepped through the back door of *AMERICAN FEDERATION OF MUSICIANS LOCAL #535* and out into what was fast becoming daybreak it was clear they wouldn't be able to make it too much further.

"Let me give you a hand." It was the leader, Fraser's tour guide, the trumpet player, the man as yet unnamed.

"Shit Webb! Get the fuck out of here, we'll get home just fine without your fucking help."

Fraser was less sure that he'd be able to get J. J. home and thankful that Webb ignored Johnson's rebuffing. Fraser took Johnson's right arm around his shoulder, Webb the left, and the three made their way through the waning hours of the night towards J. J.'s home. For the most part, Johnson was quiet save for the occasional grunt or 'shit' or 'shut the fuck up.' For the most part, he just hung his head down as the two younger men led the way.

"How long you been playing that thing?" Webb started.

"Not long, I played violin before, for years now, but I don't play that at all anymore."

"I should say not. Shit, look at your hands, how did you ever work your way around a violin with those huge hands?

"I did alright," Fraser smiled to himself.

"Anyway, you sure played the shit out of everyone tonight." Webb was genuinely impressed.

"Thanks man, sometimes it just comes easy." It had come easy.

It wasn't until that moment that Fraser had taken the time to even think about the events of the past evening. A few hours ago he had been in his usual spot, taking in what had been forbidden. Looking at the apple hanging on the tree. With the blink of an eye, the beat of a heart, the apple was pulled down, thrust into his mouth and before he could pull away, his teeth had sunk in and there was juice dripping down his chin onto his clothes.

"You should come with me to New York," Webb's voice startled Fraser back to the street.

"I should do what, with who now?" Fraser's words ran into one another.

"Shit man, you should come with me to New York. I'm just passing through here. Me and the other boys you played with tonight have a couple of dates nearby, then one or two in Chicago, and then a week in New York. I've got a couple of women we can stay with while we're there. I may even stay longer if things work out alright."

Fraser couldn't go anywhere and the only woman he could stay with was his Mother and "Shit, I didn't realize it was so late. There's J. J.'s place up ahead, do you think you can make it the rest of the way yourself?"

"Got some piece of ass waiting on you at home?"

"No, I've just got to go."

"Well think about it boy. I'll be around a day or two if you want to go, but don't wait too long. I may be gone tomorrow and who knows when you'll see Webb's fine self around here..."

Fraser missed the last few words. He was off and running. Not to New York, but to the corner of 12th and Cottonwood. He was regularly coming home in the small hours of the morning, but this was the first time the sun had beaten him into their apartment.

He ran the whole way. As he turned the corner from Cottonwood to 12th and then the quick corner to the stairway leading up to the second floor he suddenly came to an abrupt stop. A force moving almost as fast as him was moving in the opposite direction.

"Peterson, what the fuck are you doing here?" For a moment, Fraser was back at Hall #9 with Gladys. In just as quick an instant he was back, at daybreak with Mr. Peterson standing between he and his Mother.

"You're even talking like them now, and after all we did for you, going off and pissing it all away. Don't worry, I'll fill Clayton in and you'll never make a dime in this town again. You had better get your sorry ass upstairs. Your mother does not deserve such an ungrateful little shit of a son as you, after all she's done for you..."

Fraser pushed Peterson aside. Hard. Peterson fell backwards gasping in shock and/or pain. Fraser didn't stick around to see if he had done any damage.

"Mom?" Fraser tentatively poked his head through the door leading into the living room. The radio was on.

"W.B.E.Z. presents, live from the Royal Roost in the one and Only New York City, the Miles Davis Nonet, arrangements by Gil Evans . . ."

"Who is she?" his Mother's voice was just above a whisper. "I just want to know her name. Mr. Peterson was kind enough to come all the way up here and tell me what was going on. I just want to know what her name is."

"What whose name is Mother? I don't know what you're talking about."

"I could handle the dropping out of school. I could handle the staying out late. You're just a boy, I kept reminding myself that. I kept telling myself that it was for your music. Now, I found out your violin has been sitting on in a room at the hall, untouched for days, sometimes weeks at a time and you're off doing who knows what."

"Mother, you've got it all wrong."

"I do, do I? Mr. Peterson followed you the other day. Since you don't know where you went, I'll tell you. You went to that old whorehouse over by the old station house. I thought that place had closed down, but I guess you had no trouble finding it."

The woman sitting in front of Fraser wasn't his Mother any longer. Was this the heart break they both knew was coming?

"Mom, I was there but . . ."

"I know you were there. Please don't lie about what you were doing. I'm not stupid. I just thought I had raised you better than to abandon me for some cheap, black whore."

It was hopeless Fraser thought. I'll explain J.J. and the bass and all the new music I'm playing in the morning. "I'm going to bed," he said.

"NO!" She screamed. The next words out of her mouth were distant, but precise. "This is not your home any longer. Get your things and get out. I can't go through it again. I won't go through it again. Get your things and get out."

She was right. Fraser knew this was right. He went to his room, gathered as much as he could carry, went through to the kitchen, got an old cloth sack, put his belongings in and left through the front door for the last time.

"Thank you and now, featuring Lee Konitz on Alto Sax another Evans arrangement of the classic tune by Delange and Van Heusen, 'Darn That Dream.' "Darn That Dream I dream each night..."

The song carried Fraser out and into the new day and his Mother back to the old.

THIRD SET

I. Fraser lost track of time. At first, he wandered the streets not sure where he was heading. Eventually, the sun well up by now, he found himself in front of J. J.'s., Webb was coming up the stairs of Johnson's apartment.

"Shit boy, you don't want to go down there," he said.

Webb's words startled him and he didn't really hear them. "What?" he managed to say.

"You really don't want to go down there," Webb said. "It's not pretty. Your man took it a little too far after we got home last night."

Fraser heard him this time but ignored the warning and went down, two steps at a time.

James Johnson sat propped up in the corner. He actually looked much the same way he had looked the night before when he was sitting in a chair propped up against the wall. This time there was no chair. Johnson was on the cold, hard floor. The needle was still stuck in his left arm, the belt pulled tight around his bicep. Fraser stood in the doorway simply staring. He heard Webb come down the stairs behind him.

"Did you fucking do this to him?" a dark, low growl came from the boy.

"Shit, no. I just found him like this. We did a little last night after I got him home, but he was still breathing when I fell asleep.

Shit, it's a shame, best damn bass player I've played with. Where'd you take off to last night anyway?"

Fraser ignored Webb, went over to J. J. and sat down beside him on the floor.

From the moment he picked himself up off J. J.'s floor and followed Webb up the stairs, up into the daylight, time didn't move the same way it had before. It was as if Fraser were looking at someone else's life. The feel of the air against his skin changed. Even though his arm was bare, it felt like a thin cotton sleeve insulated him from the elements. The sounds entering his ears sounded distant, even if they were right beside him. Crimson now looked merely red.

And then there was Webb.

His real name was Herbert A. Davis but everybody, and I do mean everybody, called him Webb. When he was around seven or eight years old, Herbert A. Davis turned into Spider. They started calling him Spider because he was long and spindly, like a spider, small body, all arms and legs. He liked it when people called him Spider. Spiders were scary, mysterious creatures who could sneak up behind you, crawl up your back, into your hair, and mess you up before you'd even know they were there. Spider fancied that idea. He would practice that art as a small-time crook around his neighbourhood. In truth his older sister, who had given him his nickname, called him Spider because she had wanted to crush him and his annoying, obnoxious, little brother ways, under her foot, like a real spider.

A natural talent, who could do just about anything he set his mind to, Spider latched onto music and started playing trumpet. Success came easy. One day on a gig, he heard about this guy named Chick Webb, who 'lead a killer group in New York' and so changed his name to Webb. Maybe someone would mistake this Webb for 'the' Webb. He planned to use that to his advantage.

Fraser followed Webb quickly away from J. J.'s. They went straight to the A. F.of M. #535, picked up J.J.'s bass and the three other players from the night before. Fraser didn't recognize the other players even though he had played with them just a few hours ago.

"Time to go boys," was all Webb said. The other three dropped what they were doing, packed up their stuff and headed out the door. There was no real rush, but they didn't take their time either.

The instruments and suitcases were packed into a trailer. The five musicians rode together in a blue and white, late model sedan. Fraser didn't know the make or model. He never could remember stuff like that. All he could remember were colours and shapes and sounds. If the car had been black, this would have been a repeat of the night he piled into the car with four other musicians and headed to the *Cherry Hill Social Club* with Mr. Peterson in the front seat and three mysterious dark shapes around him.

But that trip was at night. This trip started out in bright daylight.

There was little conversation, or at least little that Fraser was aware of as the car pulled out of the city into the countryside that quickly surrounded the car and its occupants. Fraser had purposefully closed his eyes as the scenery began to get unfamiliar. The next thing he knew, the car had come to a stop. Night had fallen and he didn't recognize any of the buildings, streets or signs that were all around him.

He stepped out of the car, the others had just done the same, his head seemed to spin all the way around his body. It was as if his body was still moving and all the bright lights and sights and sounds were rushing past.

"Is this New York?" Fraser's mouth was dry and he hardly made it through the sentence.

"Hey Webb," one of the musicians, maybe the piano player, called out. "The boy wants to know if this is New York."

Webb laughed, "No man, we're nowhere near New York. Tonight, we play here."

Fraser looked over to where Webb was standing. A long, narrow flight of stairs lead down to what Fraser assumed was a door. There was no marking above or around the door, save for a small handwritten sign that read: *"Tonight: ***Webb's All-star Revue***."*

For a moment Fraser wonder who the All-stars were.

Then a voice behind him said, "Hey man, get your ass back here and help us carry this shit in." Fraser almost went back to the car for his violin case but he caught himself and went to the trailer where J.J.'s bass waited for him.

Everything was moving far too fast. It was as if in only an instant his mother and J.J. had never existed and Fraser was supposed to just go on and play. Webb didn't seem to be bothered by any of the events of earlier in the day. It was just business as usual. For Fraser, maybe it was too soon. He had left his Mother and Johnson that very same day, yet the thought of either of them not being here had yet to enter Fraser's mind.

The band loaded the gear in and Fraser to set up his gear ??(this was now his bass), got a stand, a chair to lean against during breaks, water, a towel for his hands and face as if this was the millionth time he had done it. In fact, it was his first. His first as the bass player. His first in a strange town, with new musicians. His first with no net below to catch him, should he fall, even just a bit.

The rest of the band set up their instruments, readied their spaces. People filed in slowly. Before long it was time to play.

With the first note, everything came crashing down.

The strings felt like razor blades beneath Fraser's fingers. The sound coming out of his hands was like metal against metal. His hands flew off the strings and he looked around, expecting someone to be hurling something at him.

"What are you doing? Shit man, don't stop now!" It was the drummer.

"How could he want me to keep playing?" Fraser thought. "Couldn't he hear how terrible it sounded?"

Fraser started up again. The pain was worse than the first time. He looked towards the drummer as if to say, "See, you don't want me to play do you?"

The drummer looked pissed off but as Fraser continued, a smile slowly crept across his face and he nodded his head. As the drummer looked away from Fraser, he said, "That's it boy, just keep it up like that."

Fraser looked around the room. Everyone else seemed lost. The other musicians and Webb were lost in their sound. The patrons, quickly filling up the place, were lost in their conversations or their drinks or the sound in the room. Everyone was so lost in their own worlds that they could not hear the terrible sounds coming from *his* world.

Fraser may have been hitting all the right notes but they sounded terrible to him.

He didn't think he could continue. After only a few minutes the pain had spread from his fingertips, which by this point had become numb, down through his wrists, his arms, through his shoulders and was branching out into his brain and down his spine.

Just when his whole body seemed consumed by the searing, burning pain and he figured he would pass out, a wave of pins and needles ran over his body, leaving numbness behind. The whole time this was going on, Fraser continued to play.

The closest sensation Fraser could think of to describe what had happened was to liken it to water freezing. He was the water. He had gone from liquid to solid in that instant. The pain was the freezing process. "Is water still water after it has been turned to ice?" he wondered.

II. The road took them and twisted them and turned them, north, south, up, down, east, west. Fraser had no idea what direction he was traveling in. Not that it mattered. He was a shell. He was the air inside his bass, stale, old, the air from smoky dance clubs and dark halls. The air trapped inside a wooden coffin.

Every town had its people. People would come up to the band after they played and either knew one of the players or pretended like they knew one of the players. Fraser would notice that often money would exchange hands between some of the musicians and these people. Usually, money would go from a musician in exchange for a little bag of something or shortly after the local would leave a young woman would arrive and go off with the player.

To say Fraser was just along for the ride would be not quite right. That would imply that at some point he had chosen to go. Fraser had spent his whole life, up till this moment and beyond, acting not because he had said "yes" but because he had not said "no". And now he was off with Webb.

Although there were three other musicians with them and all those who made it their business to be seen with musicians, the only person Fraser hung on to was Webb. Webb became Fraser's life jacket. The only name Fraser would really remember later was Webb. Whether or not Webb was a connection to the past, his Mother, J. J., a father figure for Fraser, or just a familiar face, Fraser clung to him as if he would drown should Webb happen to slip out of his sight.

Webb liked the attention.

"Hey F," Webb's accent became thicker the closer to New York they got. "Hey F, come here a minute man. There is someone I would like to introduce you to.

Fraser turned from the trailer. He had just loaded his bass in and was about to lock it up for the night's drive.

"What's up Webb?"

"This pretty little lady just loved your playing tonight and she told me she would just love to take a look at the hands that could make 'that big old bass sing so sweetly'."

Fraser noticed the woman beside Webb. She was small, her hands folded in front of her light blue dress, one hand clasped in front of the other. Her eyes alternated between the pattern of her dress and Fraser.

"Well don't just stand there boy. Get your ass over here." Webb's voice had a mischievous tone Fraser had never really noticed before.

"Go on girl," Webb gave the woman just the slightest push in Fraser's direction.

"My name is Tina," the girl spoke, timidly but not without some intensity. She had gone over to Fraser. He was still standing at the trailer.

"Uh, hello, my name is Jon."

"They told me your name was Fraser."

"That's just what everybody calls me. It's my last name actually, my real name is Jon."

"That's nice. I like Jon better anyway."

There was an awkward silence. Then the girl spoke.

"Well, I don't really do this, I was just out with my girlfriends and I couldn't take my eyes of you while you were playing. They told me to go talk to you, but when I went to try and find you, you had already gone outside." Her voice grew more and more relaxed as she spoke. Fraser noticed the softening and relaxed himself.

"That was when," she continued, "your friend Webb came up and asked me who I was looking for. I told him you so he brought me out here."

Fraser looked up at her. She was a little taller up close then she had appeared from a distance. Her skin was almost light, not quite dark. Her hair, a dark auburn bun pulled back tightly on her head. She wore a little make-up, all Fraser noticed were the red lips and her sparkling green eyes. Her eyes pulled down just a little at the edges making them look almost oriental.

A bit too long of a silence hung between them.

"Would you like to go someplace and maybe get a cup of coffee or something?" she asked.

Fraser was startled by the question. "No, I think we've got to get going."

Webb had crept up on the couple. He was close enough to hear what was going on, but not close enough to be noticed.

At this point, he jumped in, "OK, Fraser, don't worry about a thing. We've all got *plans* here. Why don't you go off with this nice young lady? The rest of the guys are meeting back here for breakfast mid-morning or so. You run along now, I'm sure Tina will take real good care of you."

Fraser was speechless, "All right then." He turned back to Tina and the two walked around to the front of the building.

III. "Is this where you wanted to go?" Fraser motioned to an all-night café about half a block away from the hall they had played at earlier that evening.

Tina seemed surprised, "Yea, a cup of coffee might be nice."

Fraser had had a couple of girlfriends in high school. But the girls quickly lost interest in him when they realized they would be a distant second to his music. He often noticed other musicians disappearing with girls or even women after gigs or during breaks. Obviously, he knew what they were doing, but it never really entered his mind to try it himself. Whenever a situation like this had presented itself before he had always managed to get out of it one way or another.

The two took a booth near the back. There were a few others in the restaurant but they didn't notice the musician and his 'girl' making their way to the back of the room.

Fraser let Tina led. She sat down. He sat across the table from her. They faced each other silently. A waitress approached, "Coffee," she said. It was not a question, hardly even a statement.

"Yes, please." Fraser and Tina spoke in unison.

The waitress disappeared. She didn't ask if they wanted anything to eat. They would have said no anyway.

"Everybody was really listening to you in there tonight." Tina reached across the table and grabbed Fraser's hands. "Most of the time people here just go out to drink or dance, but tonight they really listened."

Jon was nervously rubbing his hands together, working out a little stiffness in his left-hand fingers. His index finger on his right hand hurt a little as well. It had a thick callus built up on it, but he had played a little harder than usual tonight and had rubbed it a little raw.

"Oh, come on, you're just saying that. I haven't played anything worth listening to for months now."

"No, really, I think every woman in there had a crush on you tonight. Everyone thought you were playing for them, but I knew you were playing just for me."

Fraser grew suspicious. He hadn't been playing for anybody tonight. He pulled his hands away.

The coffee came. The waitress didn't offer cream. There was sugar on the table. Both reached for it. Tina grabbed it first.

"Listen," Fraser said, "I don't know if Webb put you up to this or not and I am flattered, but I don't think..." Tina cut him off.

"Is that what you think?" Her voice raised with just the right amount of indignation. The waitress looked up from behind the counter. "Do you think I'm on off those girls who just goes after whatever musician happens to be in town?" She did not lower her voice.

Fraser looked up at her. Her face a mixture of hurt and disdain. He believed her. He fell in love.

92

"Is this boy bothering you?" The two turned to see a large black man in a cook's apron towering over them. "You better watch how you treat a lady, boy, or I'll take you out back and teach you some manners."

"That's all right," said Tina. "I'm on my way home."

"No, wait." Fraser reached out his right hand and grabbed Tina's left shoulder, stopping her from leaving.

"I'm sorry," he said. "It's just that..."

This time the cook stopped him. "It's just that you are a stupid ass white fool who don't know a good thing when you got it." He turned to Tina, "Do you want me to get rid of this piece of trash for you?"

Tina paused for a moment. It seemed like two moments to Fraser. "No, I think we understand each other now."

They did.

"I've got my eye on you boy," the mountain of a man said as he retreated back to the kitchen.

"I'm sorry," Fraser managed. "It's just that I see all the other guys..."

"Well, I don't think that you are one of the 'other guys' and I am certainly not one on the 'other girls' or we would not be here tonight. How's your coffee?" Tina had grabbed Fraser's hand from her shoulder. She held it in both of hers.

Fraser took his first sip. "Terrible." He grimaced trying to keep it down.

"Mine too," she replied. "Let's get out of here."

Fraser got up, then remembering the coffee, left a handful of change on the table.

They went back out into the night. The sky was beginning to lighten on the horizon. For a moment, Fraser thought it might be time to meet the rest of the band.

"The sun sure comes up early this time of the year." Tina's said, her voice had lost any trace of offence. It actually sounded a little softer than it had earlier. Fraser heard the words but they drifted past him.

The sound of her voice had drawn him in. Her voice reminded him of the range between the upper end of a tenor sax and lower notes of an alto. "It was definitely a deeper sound, made high by the emphasis on the upper frequencies," he thought.

"I have an apartment near here." Tina still held Fraser's hand. "My roommate is away visiting her parents. Have you heard Miles' new album?"

"Yea, I've heard it. But I could listen to it again. If that was the only record on the planet I'd be just fine with that too." The two had already begun walking. They made their way down the street, took a right then another right then stood in front a small red brick apartment building.

"Come on, I'm on the second floor."

They made their way up the stairs. Each floor had two units. They entered the one at the top of the second-floor landing on the right-hand side. The apartment was sparse, yet functional. Four rooms, a kitchen-dining room, small living room, two doors, both open leading to bedrooms off the living room. Tina led Fraser into the living room, sat him down on a small couch and went over to a combination record player/radio that sat to the left of the couch.

"All my friends put their radios in the middle of the room. But I like it off to the side. It's just a box, you don't have to look at it to make it work." Tina took an album, the second or third from a stack of about half a dozen and placed it on the turntable. In an instant, the room was full of sound. She moved in front of Fraser and sat down on his right side. She lifted his arm, placed it around her and lay her head on his shoulder.

"Listen to this," Fraser said. "Wait for it, wait for it, there, did you hear that?"

"You mean the way the way the trumpet came in?"

"Sort of, more of the way the bass player pulls the rug out from under Miles.

Man, I can't believe that. If I ever did that to Webb, he'd go nuts. But not Miles. Listen to that. They're playing off each other. Hear how Miles is pushing him, trying to see if he can keep up?"

Tina could hear it. "Tell me more." She nestled closer into his chest.

Suddenly, Fraser couldn't think of anything more to say. He felt her slide closer to him. He accepted the weight. His eyes slipped shut. Hers did the same. The sound of the record needle bouncing against the end of the narrow groove cut into the LP's vinyl startled them both.

Tina got up. "I'll put on the radio. There are a couple of good stations here."

Fraser didn't say a word.

She flipped the switch from record to radio. It was a piano trio: drums, piano, bass. The song was slow. The drummer kept the loosest time, riding, slowly, the big cymbal on the right, the one with the rivets. The rivets bounced against the cymbal creating the gentlest of drones, a light rain shower, maybe just a mist. The piano lazily blocked out shimmering, rich chords, chords voiced high on the instrument, leaving lots of room down low for the bass. The bass filled the room, even through the small radio speaker, with warm, sweet, blankets of sound.

IV. "I'm sorry," she said. "I don't think we should have done that. You must think I am the most horrible person in the world."

They had laid quietly, without speaking for a long time. At some point, Fraser wasn't sure exactly when, they had moved from the living room to one of the two bedrooms. The sun was well up. The birds had long ago started singing. It was still relatively early though. The sleeping world was only just making its way out into the world. Soon Fraser would have to meet the rest of the band back at the parking lot.

Her voice surprised him. For a moment, he had been lost. He had drifted off. Her voice pulled him back.

"I love you," he said before he could stop the words.

"What?"

Fraser heard what he had said. "I mean I could love you, I could really love a girl like you, you're everything a guy could want, if I was your man, I could really take care of you."

"That's nice Jon." She rested back into his chest.

A few moments later, Tina pulled herself up. "You've got to get going soon. The rest of your band must be getting ready to leave by now."

Fraser didn't answer right away. His mouth opened to say 'yes' but as his lips parted, a sound entered his head. The sound wasn't a voice or words per se, but the meaning was as clear as if he had spoken them himself: *"You do not have to leave. You don't have to do anything you don't want to do. You don't owe Webb anything. You have no ties, no commitments, no obligations. You could stay right here for the rest of your life if you want to*

Fraser spoke. "Maybe I could stay here for a while."

"Aren't you going to New York?" Tina's voice revealed nothing deeper.

"I don't know. We're supposed to, but Webb keeps screwing us around, taking us all over the place. He keeps talking about New York and all the people he knows but he doesn't seem to be taking us anywhere near there." Fraser seemed to gain strength.

"I don't know," Tina added just the slightest bit of playfulness to her words. "I'm sure Webb knows what he's talking about. Besides, what would you do here? There are no players anywhere near as good as you here. Even if Webb doesn't get you to New York, you're good enough to get there on your own. Go on," she added. "I'll write to you. Maybe when you're big and famous I'll come to New York and we can paint the town red."

"But," Fraser managed.

"But nothing," she said. "You can't stay here, trust me. Go on now, get dressed, I'll make some breakfast and get you back to Webb before they take off without you."

There was no more room for debate. Fraser got up, dressed, cleaned up. Tina made toast, slightly undercooked eggs and better coffee than the café had offered the night before.

"Here," Tina handed him a piece of paper. "This is my address. You don't have to write, but there it is if you want it."

Fraser thought for a moment. He had no address to give her. "How will you get a hold of me?" he asked.

"I don't know, don't you have a home address or something?"

Fraser had none.

"Maybe I can write to the Union Hall in New York. I'm sure that will be your first stop when you get there. You can write to me here and I will write to you there. You can pick-up my letters once you arrive."

Fraser couldn't argue. This made sense. "That sounds good." He finished his breakfast.

"Don't get up," she said. "I'll take care of that." She took the plate and empty cup from in front of Fraser.

"You should get going, the rest of the band must be waiting by now."

Fraser got up. Tina put the dishes in the sink.

"Let me walk you down to the street." She wiped her hands on a dish cloth, took Fraser's hand in hers and led him out the apartment door, down the stairs and out into the morning light.

"Do you remember how to get back," Tina asked.

"There or here?" He remembered both.

"You really are great Jon Fraser." Tina looked at him a little differently. Her eyes took in more than just the man he was. She saw, for just an instant, the man Fraser had or maybe would become.

"I think I can make my way back. I'll write you as soon as I find a pencil and some paper."

"Well boys, look at what the cat dragged in." Webb was laughing as he saw Fraser turn the corner to the parking lot around back where they had left the car last night. The rest of the band hollered and cheered and made all sorts of noises Fraser had heard before, but had not participated in. His head dropped and he pulled back in on himself.

"Well Mr. Fraser, sir, give us the whole report. We've got money riding on this." Webb stood in front of Fraser, dressed in the same suit he wore on the bandstand the night before. For the first time, Fraser really looked at him. Webb had a huge grin on his face. He looked like a demon either fresh from a kill or ready to pounce.

"We just talked," Fraser lied.

"You just talked!" Webb was incredulous. "Shit boy, you just lost me fifty bucks. Just talked, shit, I should take you out back and fuck you myself, shit. Talked! Did you hear that? they just talked."

"Yea, we all heard it, now pay up sucker. I told you he was too chicken-shit to do anything." The voice came from one of the other band members.

"I'm gonna take this out of your hide boy." Webb said to Fraser as he reached into the inside pocket of his jacket and pulled out his wallet.

Fraser didn't care. "Hey Webb," Fraser said. Webb turned back toward him. "When are we going to get to New York?"

"Shit, boys do you hear that? He costs me fifty dollars and then he starts in on me about New York."

Webb sauntered up to Fraser, chuckled, looked around then grabbed by the throat and hissed into his face, "We'll get to New York when we fucking get to New York. Now shut the fuck up, get in the car and don't say another fucking word. You dig?"

He let Fraser go. Fraser fell backwards. The rest of the band was quiet. Fraser looked around, dropped his eyes back to the pavement, made his way over to the car, climbed in without another word.

V. The road continued. Up, down, around, time shifted, places melded together, faces blended into one, all faces save one.

Fraser kept his promise. As the car pulled out of the parking lot, leaving Tina behind, he asked if anybody had some paper and something to write with. The rest of the band ignored him. He didn't ask again. That evening they pulled into yet another town, yet another club. Fraser went straight to the small office, near the back door. The guy in the office looked Fraser up and down, but wordlessly handed over a few blank sheets of paper and a moderately used pencil.

Fraser thanked him, then just before turning, stopped and added, "Oh, I need an envelope too. If you've got one."

The man answered, "Get the fuck out of here kid, I'm busy. Get an envelope at the post office. Who do you think I am, your goddamn personal mailman?"

Fraser didn't care. His shoulders shrugged and he laughed to himself as he turned and went back to help unload the gear from the small trailer, in tow behind the long black car.

That night, everything changed.

It started slowly, building gradually yet consistently. It started in Fraser's chest, just to the left side of his heart, where that tight little ball of pain had nestled itself. Fraser had stopped noticing the little aches, pains, tightness, and twinges. The little ball started loosening a little. The ball then worked its way out to center of his chest, just below the surface of his skin. Fraser closed his eyes.

The rest of the band was playing hard, a fast 'Rhythm Changes' in E flat. Not a bad trumpet key and Webb was playing it for all it was worth. The tune ended just as Fraser's eyes closed and that little ball started applying pressure just below the surface of his chest.

Before Webb could call out a new number, Fraser started. A slow Blues in B flat. The first note started up in the rafters somewhere, floating around, looking for a place to come in. It came in through the top of Fraser's head, down through his body and saw a weak spot where that little ball of pain was starting to push at his chest. The big, rich, all enveloping B flat saw its chance and went for it. It poured out of Fraser and washed over the rest of the room, changing all it covered (and it covered everything) from red to blue.

Immediately after the B flat, the little ball of pain made its way out of Fraser and into the world. Fraser followed both these things. He followed them out into the world. He let them lead his fingers around his bass. He let them lead the sound wherever it was they wanted to take it.

The crowd didn't know what hit them. First, they were stunned to silence by this overwhelming sound. It was as if they were under water or submerged in a warm, thick liquid that not only allowed them to breath, but nourished them as well. This warm, thick embrace encapsulated them first, but then they were hit full-force with all the pain, hurt, struggle that followed.

The rest of the band followed Fraser as well. They had no choice. The rest of the band that is, except for Webb. Webb resisted. The B flat had hit him, too, but to him it felt more like a slap on the back of the head. He turned around to see Fraser, lost to the world, lost in his own world, put his horn to his lips and tried to blow. He tried to blow but his sound was lost in Fraser's.

When it was done, the crowd was quiet for what seemed like an eternity. Perhaps it was. Then, an explosion of sound erupted. Normally, the musicians would have been surprised, but on this night, this was the only possible reaction.

Fraser, for his part, just opened his eyes and smiled. He had played. He had played for his Mother, for his Father, for J.J., for everyone, for himself. He had wrapped up all those people and all those things into a bow he would call Tina and he had played for her.

The crowd would not let Fraser go. The band played for hours. Word spread and soon the club seemed to have tripled its capacity. Had they stopped immediately after Fraser's Blues, Webb would have gone up to Fraser and, who knows what he would have done. But, the night continued and after a few more songs Webb, had convinced himself that the rest of the crowd was there because of his trumpet playing.

VI. The group was inspired. All were inspired by Fraser, except for Webb. Webb thought he was everyone's source of inspiration. And Tina was Fraser's muse. He played for her. Each night, when his eyes would close, he reached out to her with his music. The first thing he noticed was that he had never played for anyone before. He hadn't even played for himself. With Tina in his mind, his fingers moved of their own accord. Rather than try and control his hands, he let them go. And they went.

Days turned into weeks, weeks into months. Finally, Webb walked into the greasy little restaurant where the rest of the band had already ordered their lunch and announced: "Well boys, here we go. I just got off the phone with Kenny Clark and he said that he could book us into his club. Hey Fraser, do you know where his club is?"

Fraser said nothing.

"His club is in New York City. Shit, you guys owe me big for this one, especially you Fraser. None of you would have gotten to New York unless you were riding on my coattails. I can see the sign now, *'THE GREAT WEBB'* in big, bold letters. I'll make sure they add *'and his band'* somewhere on the marquee."

Webb laughed loudly. Every head in the diner turned to look. The other musicians chuckled. Once again, Fraser said nothing.

"What's wrong, boy?" Webb pulled up a chair next to Fraser. Webb's accent was fully New York now. "I thought you would be pissing in your chair when you found out I was taking you to New York."

"I'm pissing on the inside," Fraser replied without looking Webb in the eye. It struck Fraser as odd, hadn't this whole trip been about getting to New York? Why was Webb making it sound like this was a new thing?

Webb laughed loudly again. "Shit boy, you're getting weirder every day. You're the luckiest bastard of them all, that I let you play with me."

Word had spread about Webb's group. The jazz world was tight and when something big was happening, people were quick to jump on the bandwagon. Word had begun to spread before Fraser met Tina, but afterward it spread like wildfire. The script went something like this:

"Did you see those guys downtown last night?" a member of the previous night's audience would say.

"No," the intrigued friend or co-worker would reply.

"Well, they got this motherfucker of a bass player. I heard he swung so hard one night that the walls cracked and the roof almost caved in."

"Shit, what's his name?

"I don't know, but the leader is some guy named Webb. I thought it was Chick Webb at first, you know what great players he always gets, but then I heard it was this other guy. Shit, he probably just stole Chick's name to sell seats. Anyway, if you get a chance, check it out, the bass player is unbelievable."

The long blue and white car with the trailer in tow pulled into New York City just after sunset. The day was cloudy, but warm. People were ready for a show.

"Are we stopping by the Union Hall to pick up our work cards?" Fraser sat in his usual seat, behind the driver, against the back door. He had lost count of the letters he had sent Tina.

"No," one of the other musicians answered. "Didn't you hear Webb?" He took on his best fake New York accent. Webb didn't notice the sarcasm. *"We are so damn important that the Union rep is meeting us at Kenny's to give us our cards in person."*

Fraser looked around in slight panic as the car crossed the bridge. Then a breath. Tina's letters could wait a little while longer.

Kenny Clark's was pretty much like any other club in any other city. It was a little smaller though, much dirtier and smelled worse than Fraser had expected. Fraser didn't notice much of this, however. He wasn't noticing much at all.

After a quick set up, waiting, and a couple of hours watching Webb doing his best peacock imitation, Kenny came backstage and said, "All right boys, time to go. Webb's already out there."

Fraser made his way up and onto the small stage. He took his usual place, left of the drums. A small scattering of applause rose from a larger group.

Webb began. Facing the band, he said in his best bandleader bravado, "AH, THERE YOU ARE. IT IS SO NICE OF YOU TO JOIN ME."

Turning to the crowd, he continued, "LADIES AND GENTLEMEN PLEASE JOIN ME IN WELCOMING THE BEST GROUP OF MUSICIANS I COULD FIND (under the circumstances) TO JOIN ME ON THIS HISTORIC OCCASION."

From the back of the room, a real New York accent shouted, "Shut up and play!"

Webb responded, "WELL, I CAN SEE YOU CAN WAIT NO LONGER SO WITHOUT FURTHER ADIEU, I THANK YOU FOR COMING AND I SHALL BEGIN."

Webb jumped up onto the small stage. "OK boys, don't fuck up."

Drums began, a fast blues.

From the first note, Fraser knew something was wrong. The pain was back. The pain he hadn't felt for months. The pain that had left, chasing after that low B flat. The pain was back with a vengeance. He wasn't sure where it had entered this time, but it swelled up in his guts and made its way up. Up into shoulders, down his arms, to his hands and "No, not onto my bass!" his voice screamed inside his head.

He stopped it. Fraser stopped the pain from working its way out of his fingers, into his instrument and out into the world. He kept it inside. It retreated into a thick knot which covered both his shoulder blades before it finally settled into his right side.

108

All he could think to do was play from the pain.

His eyes rolled back. His head followed, "Think only about the pain," the voice in his head said. "Focus, see the pain." Was it J.J.'s voice?

The more he thought, the more intense the pain got. He had to stop. How could anybody play like that?

Slowly his playing shifted from blue to red. The lines got sharper. His fingers dug in. He was going now. Two choices: let the pain use him or he use the pain. He was going now. Further and further down, then up, in, then out.

His eyes now closed tight. His mind off in space, the walls drifted away, the other players drifted away, the crowd, the stage, drifted away. Only his mind and the pain. Suddenly, the pain too drifted away, out of his back and right in front of him. Staring at him, big, green, menacing. Standoff: him reddish orange - it green and dark. Suddenly, the two merged, violently. He took off. The sound became dangerous.

The battle raged on. He was lost in the pain the pain was lost in him. Then the voice came back, clear, loud to Fraser.

"Don't go back," the voice told him. "Stay here with me."

"But I have to," he replied, "I don't belong here."

Fraser had gone somewhere he had never gone before. J.J. hadn't prepared him for this, no one had.

"Everyone belongs here, this is the only place that's real." The voice continued.

The other players played on. Feeding off his intensity, oblivious to the path he was taking them down.

"Not yet," he pleaded, "I can't go yet."

His head suddenly dropped back down, eyes popped open. He heard the band again for the first time since closing his eyes. They were on fire. Firing on all cylinders. They were about to explode.

"That's it, I've got to slow this thing down," he thought. "Pedal the root. Pedal the root. Pedal the root and we're done ...but no, that stupid bastard Webb was outlining the wrong chord. That goddamn son of a bitch."

They all looked around in amazement. Where had they just gone?

"That's the wrong fucking chord," Fraser said it loud enough for everyone to hear.

"What did you say?" Webb fired back.

Fraser was in trouble. He didn't speak.

"What did you say!?" no longer a question from Webb.

Quietly, "You ended on the wrong notes."

The crowd was quiet now as well, Webb looked around, shrugged his shoulders and shuffled over to him.

Webb walked slowly up to Fraser. Fraser could smell the heat on his breath. Webb had a thin layer of sweat on his upper lip that was just starting to dry.

"I played the wrong notes?"

"Yea man it's no big deal, nobody noticed, it's no big deal."

"No big deal, no big deal..."

110

Webb swung his left arm around Fraser's neck, the bass fell to the floor. His trumpet to the floor too. Webb reached into the outside pocket of his suit jacket and pulled out a small, black, snub nosed pistol. Left arm around Fraser's neck, right hand shoving the barrel of the gun in his face.

"Webb don't play no motherfucking wrong notes, you dig...?" he spit out the words, like a snake hissing before going in for the kill.

"Jesus Christ Webb, don't be an asshole," someone called out from behind.

He held him like that for a moment or two longer, then let him go. Fraser fell, just a little, stepped back and picked up the bass.

"Shit man it wasn't even loaded," Webb said as he turned to face the rest of the crowd.

"Rhythm changes in F," Fraser called out as he picked up his bass.

"Yea, rhythm changes in motherfucking F," Webb said as he made his way back to the front of the stage.

VII. The night ended. They had played until dawn. Fraser hadn't felt much of anything since Webb pulled his gun.

"Where are you going boy?"

Fraser had left his bass on the bandstand and was heading for the door. He stopped. He didn't know where he was going.

"I'm going to the Union Hall. do you know where it is?" It was the piano player who had asked the question and the piano player whom Fraser directed this question to.

"Why do you want to go there? We already got our cards." Webb was nowhere to be seen.

"I got some stuff to pick up there. Do you know where it is or not?"

"Shit, no man, I ain't never been to New York either. Hey Kenny, do you know where the hall is at man?" The piano player had turned to Kenny Clark. Clark had been seated at a table near the bar. He was counting cash.

"Who wants to go to the Union Hall?" Clark took just one eye of the thick-ish pile of bills.

"Fraser," the piano player replied.

"Fraser?" Clark turned to the bass player. "What the hell do you want there? Shit you've only been in New York for a couple of hours you think they'll be lined up to give you work already?"

"I've got some stuff to pick up," Fraser repeated.

Clark gave him directions. It was close. Fraser walked out of the club, turned left and started to run.

The Hall was closed. He walked around the nearly empty streets, stopped for coffee at two different diners and was waiting by the door when a well-dressed woman in a blue business suit unlocked the door.

"Excuse me, my name is Jon Michael Fraser. I think you have some letters for me?"

"Hang on kid," she replied. "You up early or late?" She asked as she went into the neatly furnished office and made her way behind a broad, oak reception desk.

"What makes you think we have letters for you? This is the AFofM you know, not the post office. We deal with musicians, not mailmen." Fraser was overly anxious; the secretary was playful.

"I had some letters sent to me here. There should be a bunch."

"Listen, what did you say your name was?" Fraser told her, she replied, "Well Jon Michael Fraser even if some letters did get sent here for you, if the person the mail is for doesn't work here, we send it back."

"But you've got to check, talk to the person who gets the mail."

"I'm the person who gets the mail." She was beginning to get less playful as Fraser grew more and more frantic. "I'm telling you, I would remember if a whole bunch of letters came here for you and I'm sure there weren't any."

Fraser lunged over the woman's desk. He pulled open drawers, knocked papers to the floor.

"For Christ sake, they've got to be here, is this the only Union Hall in New York, they've got to be here, what are you talking about, look for Christ sake . . ."

"Jimmy!" The secretary had gotten out of the way of Fraser and called for help. Help was on its way before she had cried out.

From out of nowhere, 'Jimmy' arrived. He grabbed Fraser, picked him up, one hand on his shirt collar, the other on his waist. Fraser was big, but Jimmy was much bigger. He had no trouble lifting the frantic bass player off the secretary's desk and throwing him cleanly out the front door.

He landed at Webb's feet.

"There you are," Webb said. "Whoa, what's going on here?"

"Shit, and here I thought you were trying to undercut me." Webb was laughing yet again. "I thought you had some inside job lined up but you were just getting yourself beat up."

Fraser hit the ground hard, his mouth was filling with blood. He tried to stand up.

"You can stay the fuck down there." Webb's foot came down hard on Fraser's shoulder. "After that stunt you pulled on the stand tonight, trying to show me up, you ungrateful shit. You belong down there with the rest of the rats. Just try to get a gig here now, after word of what you tried to pull on me last night gets around."

Fraser didn't try to fight. He let his eyes slip closed.

VIII. Two strong hands reached under Fraser's arms, rolled him over and got him into a seated position. Fraser's didn't open his eyes.

"Hey boy, you had better come to, you'll get trampled if you lay here any longer." It was Kenny Clark. He had taken Webb to the Union Hall, but not followed him when he left Fraser lying in a heap in the middle of the sidewalk.

Fraser snapped to attention. "There's got to be another hall. She must have sent the letters there." With the words came a smattering of blood.

"Easy boy." Clark put a hand on his shoulder, keeping Fraser from getting up.

"Where do you think you're going? What's the big deal with these Union Halls?"

The newfound strength left Fraser immediately. He stopped trying to fight. He told Kenny about Tina. He went on and told Kenny Clark about J.J., then about his Mother and finally about his Father; Private First Class—Michael Jon Fraser—killed in the war the day he was born. He sat there in the middle of the street and let it out. He couldn't hold it in any longer. He sat in the middle of the sidewalk in New York city. He had nowhere else to go.

"She must have sent the letters to the black hall." Fraser looked at Kenny Clark for the first time that morning.

"There is no black or white hall here, just the one you are sitting in front and we had better get moving. It's starting to get busy." Clark helped Fraser to his feet. Fraser didn't resist.

"You can come back to the club. There a couple of rooms upstairs. One of them is empty. You can stay there for a day or two, just till you get your shit together." Clark's voice reminded Fraser, only slightly, of J.J.'s. Fraser didn't turn down the offer.

The club was deserted when they got back. The two made their way through the back alley and in through the back door. Clark had a little trouble getting the key to fit in the lock. For a moment, he thought that someone had filled the keyhole with glue again.

The club was deserted save for the bass, which lay propped up against the back wall. Fraser had dropped it on the ground when he left. Someone must have moved it to its current, more noble position. Clark lead Fraser to a table at the front of the stage. Fraser sat down.

"Wait here," Clark said. "I'll get you a glass of water, or something harder if you're ready for it."

"Just water, thanks." Fraser's voice was just above a whisper. The blood had dried around his mouth and cracked when he opened his lips.

"Here." Clark threw Fraser a rag from behind the bar. "You'd better wipe your face. I think it looks worse than it is."

Clark was right. Fraser had only bitten the inside of his cheek. A fair chunk of flesh was gone but the injury was, for the most part, superficial.

"Do you know anybody in town?" Clark handed him the glass of water.

Fraser shook his head.

"I didn't think so. What's Webb up to? I just gave him the one night here. What else did he book for you guys?

Fraser just looked at Clark.

"OK, then," Clark replied. "You should get some sleep. Come on, the room is up here." He led Fraser up a flight of stairs, past an office, through a doorway that lead to a small hall. Two doors faced opposite each other on either side of the hallway.

"Take your pick," Clark said. "I lied earlier, they're both empty. The guy who owned this place before me used to do some pimping out of here, but I haven't bothered with that yet. I'm the only person who has used them for the last couple of months, only when the old lady kicks me out."

Clark smiled, Fraser just walked down the hall and took the door on the right-hand side. As he opened the door, he realized that at that moment, that man, Kenny Clark, was the only person who had ever admitted lying to him.

Fraser turned, "Thanks," he said.

"No problem, just don't go telling a whole bunch of people. I think most folks have forgotten about these rooms and I don't want to deal with a whole bunch of people doing a whole bunch of shit up here when I'm not around."

Fraser walked through the door. The room had a single bed, pressed tight against the right-hand wall (as you walked in). A lamp on a night stand stood beside the bed, a small chest of drawers, three drawers high, stood on the left walls opposite the bed. The room was a gentle blue.

He fell onto the bed and dreamed.

IX. After the second day, Kenny moved the bass up into Fraser's room. Fraser had been out of his room only a couple of times and then only to use the toilet and eat a sandwich Kenny had brought for him. The sound of the club at night hadn't even disturbed him.

For the most part, Fraser just slept. He slept and he dreamed. His dreams took him everywhere. It was all he could do to open his eyes and leave his dreams. A couple of days turned into a couple of weeks. Kenny didn't seem to mind. In truth, it was as if Fraser wasn't there. He would bring Fraser bits to eat a couple of times a day. Sometimes it would get eaten, sometimes not.

Finally, Fraser could postpone it no longer. He dreamt that J.J. had come back to him.

"Well boy, what's it gonna be?" In the dream, J.J.'s face looked different but the voice was unmistakable. "Are you gonna come with me or are you gonna stay there for a little while longer?"

In the dream, Fraser's mouth opened to speak but no words came out. Instead, a thick torrent of colour poured from him. First red, then blue, then through the entire spectrum of colours, then colours that had never existed in the waking world poured from Fraser. In his dream

He opened his eyes.

He turned his head and could only see one thing, the bass. He hadn't noticed it before, but the wood was stained an almost reddish hue. The wood seemed thicker than it had before. It was covered in nicks, scrapes, dents. Each mark was filled in and looked a little, just a shade, darker than the rest of the wood. It was as if the imperfections were alive, crawling all of the instrument, maybe playing with each other, maybe fighting. Each mark had its own story. All the marks together made this bass sing.

He sat up, a little too fast, his head spun. He waited for a moment.

He got to his feet. His legs were stiff, but steady enough.

He picked up the bass. It was still in tune.

C major to the 9th and back down: Do Re Mi Fa Sol La Ti Do Re . . . Re Do Ti La Sol Fa Mi Re Do.

His hands felt good. The calluses had thickened during his sleep.

C Seven to the 9th and back down: Sol La Ti Do Re Mi Fa Sol La . . . La Sol Fa Mi Re Do Ti La Sol.

"Any dumb fuck can go from root to root," Johnson took on his preacher voice again. "It takes a real man to go to the ninth. Listen to it," he ordered, "you just resolve it, just make it sound pretty again and then BAM, you slip past it, teasing them a bit. It's like a woman, bending over just far enough to let you see that she's got something under that shirt then standing up before you have the chance to get a real good look."

Fraser promised himself to look down more girls' tops.

"Don't think of them like scales," J.J. would continue, "think of them like chords. Follow all your chords from the root to the ninth

120

then back down. When some asshole calls out some chord changes, you got to see your neck in all different ways, different for each chord."

The words came back to Fraser's mind. Each note grew stronger than the last.

C Minor (Dorian) to the 9th *and back down: Re Mi Fa Sol La Ti Do Re Mi . . . Mi Re Do Ti La Sol Fa Mi Re.*

In an instant, the voices inside Fraser's head stopped.

Silence.

X. "Well shit, look here." Clark had opened the door. Fraser stood before him. He had his back turned to the door and all Kenny could see was Fraser's back and the bass, which Fraser's naked body did a less than adequate job of covering up.

"I thought I'd be dragging a corpse out of here. Shit boy, put some clothes on. You haven't snapped on me now have you? Fuck, I was there where Bird used to get all fucked up and crazy and I ain't doing that again."

Fraser laughed. "No, I'm all right." He hadn't noticed that he was naked. When he did, his laugh turned to a chuckle, then a soft "Shit."

"Are you back with us boy?" Clark asked as Fraser quickly pulled his clothes on. Clark had had them cleaned while Fraser slept.

Fraser thought about it for a moment, "Yea, I am."

"Do you feel like playing?"

This took less thought, no thought really, there was nothing else to do. "Yea, I am."

"I got a group coming in here tonight, their leader just called, their bass player took off on them in Chicago. He met a girl or something, shit. They asked me to find someone to sit in. Nothing too hard, just blues and a couple of rhythm changes."

"That'd be good." Fraser sat back down on the bed, fully clothed this time.

"Well, when you get your shit together, come on downstairs. They'll be here in a couple of hours. There's some food down there. You should eat. You do look like shit you know."

Fraser knew.

Clark left him and went back downstairs. The club was still empty. Fraser took a deep breath, stood up and followed.

ENCORE

There were more stories. Lots more stories. If there's one thing Fraser could do, it was tell stories, whether with his bass or over a drink. He was just a kid when Kenny Clark led him back down into the world. He hadn't even been recorded yet, not even those early Art Blakey discs.

I think he'd want me to stop here though.

"When you've played enough, when the audience has learned what you got to teach them, then it's time to shut up and move on." He told me that J.J. had told him that.

"Sometimes that's just one note, sometimes it's no notes at all," he added.

"Did J.J. tell you that?" I asked

"Shit no. I figured that one out on my own. The hard way I might add..." he said. "You're lucky I told you that. I just saved you a whole mess of heartache figuring that out for yourself."

Lucky indeed. Yup, lucky indeed.

ABOUT THE AUTHOR

Jim studied jazz guitar at Malaspina University College in Nanaimo, BC, Canada and creative writing/journalism at Thompson Rivers University in Kamloops, BC. Pretty soon after finishing his music studies he switched to Chapman Stick and bass. Currently he plays bass and Stick in the rock band DC & the Struggle and gives the occasional solo Stick performance.

His writing on music has been featured in *Bass Guitar Magazine, Canadian Musician, Music Etc.,* on CBC Radio One and various places online included www.stick.com and www.nedsteinberger.com.

This is his first work of fiction. His biographies of Emmett Chapman (*StickMan: The Story of Emmett Chapman and the Instrument He Created*) and Ned Steinberger (*Steinberger: A Story of Creativity and Design*) are currently available.

For more information please visit www.jimreilly.ca.